THE COMEBACK CHALLENGE

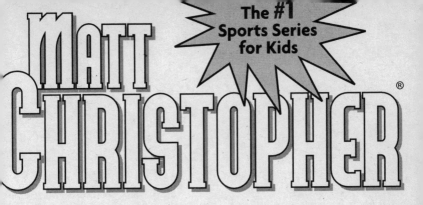

The #1
Sports Series
for Kids

MATT CHRISTOPHER ®

THE COMEBACK
CHALLENGE

LITTLE, BROWN AND COMPANY

New York ☞ Boston

Little, Brown and Company

Hachette Book Group
237 Park Avenue, New York, NY 10017
Visit our website at www.lb-kids.com

www.mattchristopher.com

Little, Brown and Company is a division of Hachette Book Group, Inc.
The Little, Brown name and logo are trademarks of Hachette Book Group, Inc.

First Paperback Edition: January 1996

Library of Congress Cataloging-in-Publication Data

Christopher, Matt.
    The comeback challenge / by Matt Christopher — 1st ed.
    p.   cm.
    Summary: Mark, center for his middle school's soccer
team, the Scorpions, must cope with his parents' divorce
and a teammate who holds a grudge against him.
        HC ISBN: 978-0-316-14090-4 / PB ISBN: 978-0-316-14152-9
    [1. Soccer —Fiction.   2. Divorce — Fiction.]
    I. Title.
PZ7.C458Cm 1996
[Fic] — dc20   95-22346

10 19 18 17 16 15 14 13

COM-MO

Printed in the United States of America

To
John, Beverly, Stephen,
Daniel, and Rachel

THE COMEBACK CHALLENGE

Rats!"

Mark Conway jiggled the window shade. It almost reached the bottom of his bedroom windowsill. Nothing happened. It wouldn't roll back up. He jiggled harder. The shade fell down on top of him.

"Stupid shade!" he muttered to himself.

"Are you all right?" came his grandmother's voice from the kitchen.

"It's this shade," he called back to her. "It won't roll up."

He heard her distant, soft laugh. "Your father used to have the same problem. You just have to roll it up by hand and put it back in the brackets. Then, when you want to lower or raise it, do it gently."

It worked. Following her instructions, Mark had the shade back and working in no time at all.

1

I would have figured it out, he said to himself.

He wandered into the kitchen. A strong scent of apples and cinnamon filled the room.

"Did you get it fixed?" his grandmother asked.

"Uh-huh," he replied.

He watched as she poured a bowl of sliced apples and sugar and spices into a round pan lined with pie dough. He reached forward, but she slapped his hand back with a laugh.

"There are some peanut butter cookies in the jar," she said, glancing over her shoulder. "This pie is for dessert tonight. Your father loves apple pie, and he might be coming over for dinner."

Mark just shrugged, but his stomach did a flip-flop. As he watched his grandmother carefully place the top of the piecrust over the apple mixture, he wondered if she knew what it was like to be stuck in the middle of a divorce. He doubted it. After all, *her* parents had stayed married. *She* hadn't been dragged all over the world when her folks' jobs had changed. And *she* hadn't had to listen to them fight over who he was going to live with — only to have a court decide that he should live with his grandparents until the divorce was settled!

To be honest, he sometimes missed the traveling. He was so young when they'd left Knightstown that the only thing he really remembered was playing soccer with the playground league. But there was a league in the seaside town on the East Coast they had moved to, and playing on the beach had been fun. He had been looking forward to starting school, too, when they packed up their bags to move to a big city a few states over. They lived there for five months before his father announced that they were off for the West Coast. Mark was happy to be out of the city, but sure enough, just when he started to pal around with a bunch of guys, his folks took him to live in England!

England! With all those kings and queens and people driving on the wrong side of the road. They had different names for things, too. When they first moved to England, they lived in a "flat" — an apartment — before they moved to their house. Even familiar food was called something else. He was always forgetting that french fries were "chips" and potato chips were "crisps."

He'd had trouble understanding the English accent at first, too. But soon he made friends and was part of a regular group of guys who went to school together and hung out together. Best yet, they all played soccer and were eager to add Mark to their team.

In fact, Mark started to like England. Too bad he had been the only one in the family who had had fun there. His folks weren't around all that much, what with their work and everything. But he had known for a long time that something was wrong between them. When winter came, the air was as frosty inside the house as it was outside.

When his parents stopped talking to each other, Mark started spending more time with his new friends. His parents didn't seem to notice that he wasn't around the house as much. But he had the bad luck to be home when the big blowup came.

Even though he was up in his room with his head buried in the pillow, he could hear the shouting below. He could tell that they weren't listening to each other. They were too busy saying all the hurtful things they had kept bottled up inside over the past weeks. Then, finally, a door slammed.

The next morning, his father wasn't at breakfast.

Mrs. Conway said that Mr. Conway was going to be living in a flat for a while. Mark would be spending weekends with him, she told him, "until they figured out what was going to happen next."

What happened next was the worst two weeks of Mark's life. He seesawed between his parents. That first weekend, Mark's father took him to a carnival that had set up in the next town. There were lots of rides and games to play, but they didn't really seem that much fun to him.

When he got home, his mother told him they were going out to his favorite restaurant. But he could only pick at his meal.

In the middle of the following week, a new video game came in the mail from his father. But his mother said he was spending too much time in front of the TV and wouldn't let him use it. Instead, she took him out to dinner again.

That's when she told Mark that his father wanted him to come and live in his flat with him. "But of course that's out of the question," she said before Mark even had a chance to react. "You'll stay in the cottage with me."

Soon after that night, lawyers began visiting both locations. They tried to get Mark to say he preferred living with one parent over the other.

The whole situation made Mark's insides turn over. How could he choose one parent without feeling disloyal to the other? So instead of sorting out his feelings, Mark just clammed up.

Then Mrs. Conway announced that she had arranged for a job transfer. She was moving back to America — and taking Mark with her. But his father wasted no time in moving back, too. The fight over who he'd live with just shifted across the ocean.

The Conway family finally found themselves in front of a judge. From behind his desk, he listened to everything they and their lawyers had to say. When they were done talking, he picked up a letter from his desk.

"This is from Mark's grandparents," he said. "They are concerned with how Mark is being affected by his parents' situation and so have offered to take Mark until this matter is settled. In my opinion, Mark has been shuttled from place to place long enough. Therefore, unless either side can come up with a better solution in the next two minutes, I am going to grant temporary custody to the Conway Seniors."

So, here he was, back in Knightstown, living with Grandma and Grandpa Conway.

They were really nice, but they were . . . well, they were *old*. And they lived in a part of town where it seemed as though there weren't any other young people.

So what was he supposed to do with himself? School was going to begin in a few days. That would be tough, Mark knew. Although he had once lived in Knightstown, he didn't really remember anybody. In all likelihood, his classmates would have known each other for years. Would they have room for a newcomer?

This would be his first year in a middle school, and already he wasn't too thrilled with it. He'd been over for registration with Grandpa Conway a few days ago, and the place was *huge*. Even if he did make friends, how would he ever find them in such a place?

He and Grandpa had stood in lines for most of the

morning, filling out forms. Mark had become so confused, he almost ended up enrolling in a girls' gymnastics class.

"They have your name, and they know where you'll be living," Grandpa Conway had said. "And you're all set with your regular classes — history, math, English, and all that. They'll send you the information about the extracurricular things. You can take your time and look those over at home, then sign up once school starts."

Since then, there really hadn't been much to do around the house. Grandpa Conway was retired, but he did volunteer work at the courthouse every day. Grandma worked mornings at the bank just down the street. When she was home, she was busy with housework and didn't have all that much time for him.

So Mark went for long walks by himself. But it had rained the last few days, and he hadn't been able to go out much. Instead, he just moped around the house. Fixing that broken shade had been the most exciting thing he'd done since Tuesday!

"Stir crazy," he announced, helping himself to a peanut butter cookie. "This must be what it's like."

"Still raining?" his grandmother asked, pinching all around the edge of the piecrust.

"Yup," he replied.

"Why don't you watch some TV?"

"Nothing on."

"What about those videos I picked up at the library?"

"Seen 'em," he said.

"Read all those books your grandfather got you?"

"All of 'em." He sighed. He didn't tell her that some he had read before because they were used in classes at his last school.

"Well, maybe when I get everything ready for dinner and out of the way, I'll play a game with you. Must be a whole mess of them in your daddy's closet — oh, wait a minute. I just remembered that we cleaned them out for a church rummage sale last year."

"That's all right," Mark said. "Maybe I'll just do that jigsaw puzzle I started yesterday." And finished this morning, he said to himself. But I'll take it apart, so she'll think I'm just beginning.

They were interrupted by the sound of the front door opening.

9

"Anybody home?" Grandpa Conway called. He said the same thing every day, whenever he came in, even when the lights were on and you could hear people talking.

That's what it's like living here, Mark thought ruefully. Same thing every day! That's what I'll be like after a while.

"Mail," announced Grandpa Conway, coming into the kitchen. "Here's a big fat envelope for you, Mark."

"For me?" Mark asked. His eyes lit up for the first time in days. Who had written to him? Was it one of his friends from overseas? Maybe his mother had gotten around to sending them his forwarding address, like she said she would!

He looked at the envelope. KNIGHTSTOWN MIDDLE SCHOOL, it said on the flap.

"Oh, it's that extracurricular stuff," he said, disappointed.

"Aren't you going to look at it?" asked his grandfather.

"I'll look at it later," he said. "I'm going to work on that jigsaw puzzle now."

As Mark left the kitchen, he tried to ignore the looks on his grandparents' faces.

When the phone rang a few minutes later, Mark was in the midst of searching for edge pieces of the puzzle. But he looked up when his grandfather came into the room.

"That was your dad," he said. "He can't make it for dinner on account of some work he's doing. He was on the car phone, and it started to fade just as he asked to speak to you. Said he'll call you tomorrow."

"That's okay," said Mark. His voice was expressionless.

"Say, let's take a look at that school envelope," Grandpa Conway suggested. "Maybe there's something we have to fill out. Might as well get it out of the way."

"Okay," said Mark. He tore open the envelope and spilled the contents out onto the table next to the puzzle. He picked up one sheet while his grandfather took another. For a moment, the two of them read quietly to themselves.

"Mine's boring," said Mark, tossing the paper aside and picking up a puzzle piece. "Just a whole lot of stuff about how we're supposed to behave ourselves when we're in school. You know, no smoking, no swearing, and all that."

"Guess I got the good part," said Grandpa Conway. "Here's a whole bunch of things you can sign up for outside of your regular classes. There's the school newspaper, the glee club, and all the team sports."

Mark wasn't much interested in the paper or the glee club. But his ears perked up at the word "sports."

"What kind of sports do they have?" he asked.

"Let's see, there's basketball, and football, and track, and gymnastics, and soccer, and swimming, and —"

"Soccer! Hah, England's where they really know how to play that!" said Mark.

"Is that a fact?" his grandfather asked, smiling. "Did you play when you lived over there?"

"Everybody played soccer," said Mark. "It's like . . . like baseball over here. Good thing I'd already played a lot before I got there!"

"You did?" His grandfather pretended not to know what he was talking about.

Mark grinned. "As if you don't remember sitting

in those playground bleachers twice a week, cheering me on!"

"It kind of comes back to me," said Grandpa Conway.

"Come on! That's when Mom was one of the coaches. It took her all season, but she finally got us to understand the importance of staying in our own positions on the field. Before, we would all just run after the ball, one big clump of five-year-olds!" Mark laughed out loud at the memory.

Grandpa laughed, too. "Then maybe you ought to go out for the school team," he suggested. "Doesn't sound like you'd have too much trouble making it onto the squad."

"You think so?" Mark said. His eyes sparkled as his grandfather gave him the thumbs-up sign. "I might just do that."

After dinner, Mark made a note of when soccer try-outs began and talked to his grandmother about arranging for him to get the physical exam required by the school. As he lay in bed that night, he felt happier than he had for weeks. At last, he had something to look forward to!

He remembered the first time he'd played soccer. The field had looked so big! But soon it was no more than a blur beneath his feet. Once he'd gotten the hang of it, he felt completely at ease dribbling, controlling, and kicking the ball through the grass. And when he scored his first goal, he had been so excited that he'd jumped up and down — and his mother, coaching from the sidelines, had shouted his name and beamed with pride.

Mark couldn't help smiling at this memory. But his smile faded at another, less pleasant memory: the time his father had accused his mother of ignoring this part of Mark's life in favor of her new career.

"You don't even know if he's playing soccer or tiddlywinks anymore!" his father had shouted.

"I certainly do!" his mother had shot back. "After all, I was the one who spent all those hours on the field! Don't you dare suggest that just because I don't have time now to be his coach means I don't have time to take care of him by myself!"

"Oh sure, when you're not busy trying to be the best salesperson in the entire world!"

"A job I'm very lucky to have, considering how many times we had to move for *your* career! Are you going to tell me that that's been good for Mark? Or that if he lives with you, that will change? Ha!"

Back and forth the argument had gone — and all the while Mark had sat in his bedroom, his fingers stuffed into his ears to keep the shouting out.

Now, as Marked snapped off the light next to his bed, he wished for the thousandth time that his parents would stop using him as ammunition against each other. But he knew that as long as their divorce was still being settled, anything he did with them or said to them was likely to become another bullet in their war.

So I guess I'll just have to watch what I do and say, he thought as he drifted off to sleep.

2

The first tryout for the Knightstown Middle School soccer team, the Scorpions, took place the same day classes started. Mark could hardly wait for the school day to be over and for the practice to begin. His classes sped by him as though they were on fast forward. When he tried to put his new books away in his locker and get out his gym bag, he was so excited, it took him three tries to make the combination work.

But after changing into his workout clothes and running out onto the field, he suddenly felt a strange, cold shiver run through his body. A large crowd of boys was already scattered on the field warming up. Many of the players seemed to know each other. He knew no one. There were several balls being kicked around, but none rolled near him. He was an outsider — and there was no guarantee, even if he made the team, that that would change.

A whistle interrupted his dismal thoughts. Coach Ryan, a tall man with steely gray hair and deep brown eyes, called out, "Okay, everyone, I want to see you form three lines: one to my right, one to my left, and one down the middle. Let's see some straight passing, lane to lane."

Within a few seconds, the whole group was caught up in the drill.

Mark started out in the middle. The player on his left dribbled the ball a few feet, then passed it over to Mark. Mark stopped it with his right foot and dribbled a few feet. Then he nudged it to the player on his right, a redheaded kid whose face was completely covered with freckles. The kid grinned at him — and for a split second, something about him seemed familiar to Mark.

But he didn't have time to think about that now. The redhead was passing the ball back to him. Again, Mark stopped it, this time with his left foot, and dribbled a few feet before passing to the player on his left. One more pass back left Mark with the ball in front of the goal. Without thinking, he swung his leg back and booted the ball solidly between the posts.

"Good work!" called the coach. "Let's see you other teams doing the same thing!"

Embarrassed at the thought that he'd looked overeager, a "coach's pet," Mark turned to jog back into line with his head down.

"I see you still have that strong kick!"

Mark looked up quickly and saw the redhead flash him a grin before sprinting away to rejoin his line.

Who's that? Mark wondered. He seems to know me — and he looks familiar to me, too. Must be in some of my classes.

But he couldn't put a name with the face. Still, the boy's friendliness cheered him up.

More important, getting back into the playing groove was making him feel more at ease. When the coach changed the straight-down-the-line drill to a three-man-weave, Mark had no trouble keeping up. He even shot on goal a few more times.

Soon after that drill, the coach broke the boys up into groups of offense and defense. Two offensive players brought the ball down the field against one defending player. The trick was for the offensive players to keep the defender from stealing the ball. Quick passes and fast footwork were key to getting by safely.

Mark started out on offense. Unsure of his partner's ability, he decided to try outsmarting the defense by himself. He dribbled straight at the defensive player. Then, when the man rushed him, he pulled the ball to one side with a swift move. The defender couldn't change direction in time. Mark dribbled by him a few feet.

"Sweet move, but the purpose of this drill is to learn to work with your teammates. Next time, try remembering that you're not alone on the field."

Mark looked up, surprised. His partner, a dark-haired boy, was scowling at him.

"S-s-s-orry," Mark stammered. "Here, you start off with the ball this time."

He tapped the ball to the other boy, then turned to face the defense again. As his partner dribbled slowly down the field, Mark made sure he stayed in his position, ready to receive any signal or pass the other boy might give him.

A moment later, Mark thought he saw him jerk his head to the left, as if to say Mark should cut across to receive a pass. But when Mark did just that, the dark-haired boy suddenly stopped moving. Mark couldn't stop himself. He crashed right into his partner, and both wound up sprawled on their backsides.

"What's with you?" the other boy asked angrily.

"Sorry," Mark said for the second time that day. "I read your signal wrong, I guess."

"Listen, you take the ball this time. When I take off past the defense, boot me a pass. Think you can handle that?"

Mark nodded stiffly. He didn't like the way the boy talked to him but decided to brush it off. The next few times down the field, they worked better together. By the time the coach had blown his whistle, signaling the end of the drill, they had defeated the defense six out of nine times. Yet Mark was sure the other boy was blaming the collision on him.

Well, I can't be everyone's friend, he said to himself. If he wants to hold a grudge, let him. I won't let it affect my playing.

Coach Ryan announced that a quick scrimmage would end the day's practice. Mark was chosen to be on the front line, playing left wing. To his dismay, the dark-haired boy lined up on his right in the center slot. Gritting his teeth, he reminded himself to treat the center like any other player.

At first Mark didn't see much action. But after he had moved the ball into a good position near the goal a few times, he seemed to be part of more and more plays.

Once, when Mark had the ball, the redheaded kid came up on his right side. Mark kept a close eye on him. Then, when he saw the coast was clear, he gestured with his head, swung around, and booted it over to the right-hand side of the goal. The redhead had understood his signal perfectly and was right there to stop the ball. Although he lost it a few moments later to a strong defensive attack, Mark was pleased that at least one person could "read" him.

Just then, the whistle blew. They ran off the field to let two more practice teams have their chance. On the sideline, the redhead approached Mark and said, "You don't remember me, do you? I'm Craig Crandall. We used to play together in the playground league. Where've you been since then? Where've you been playing soccer? Do you still live where you used to? Which bus do you take? Hey, that was one sweet setup — too bad I blew it. My mother drove me this morning, but I'm going to be on the Grant Street bus from now on. How about you?"

He's like a friendly puppy! Mark thought. Out loud, he laughed and said, "Wow, you sure ask a lot of questions. Let's see: I vaguely remember a kid we used to call Pepper because of all his freckles. Something tells me that kid was you! And yes, I will be taking the Grant Street bus, because I . . . I moved from where I used to live," Mark finished lamely. Although he was grateful for Craig's interest, for some reason he didn't feel like talking about what he'd been up to the past few years. Or why he was back in Knightstown. And living with his grand-parents.

Craig didn't seem to notice. "Yeah? Great! So is your mom still coaching? Boy, she sure was tough — good, I mean — but like, well, we sure learned what it meant to stay in our lanes!"

"Right, we sure did," Mark answered evasively. He didn't feel like talking about his mother any more than he did about the other stuff Craig had asked about. Luckily Coach Ryan called everyone over to the bench a few seconds later.

"Okay, guys, settle down!" he shouted. "This is

just our first day of practice, and we've got a lot of work to do before our first game. That goes for you veterans as well as the rookies. But for now, let's end today's session with some laps. Tonight, rest up, do your homework, and come to practice tomorrow ready to play some soccer. Now, hit the dirt for some laps!"

As Mark did his rounds with the others, he ran over in his mind everything that had happened that afternoon. All in all, he felt pretty good. He analyzed the way the rest of the guys had played and knew who he would pick to be on the team if it were up to him. But it wasn't. It was up to the coach.

But before the day was over, Mark had found out one thing that made him uneasy. As he was collecting his gear from his locker, he had heard one of the other players call the dark-haired boy he had collided with "Captain." Had Mark made an enemy out of the team's captain his first day on the field? And if so, how would that affect his playing time if he made the team?

3

The next day, Mark found out that Craig Crandall was in a couple of his classes — history and math. In the corridor between classes, Craig filled him in on a few things he didn't know about the Knightstown Middle School.

"Kids come here from three different elementary schools — Carter, Wolcott, and Liberty. Grant Street kids all come from Carter. We played soccer a lot there," he explained. "Last year we won the sixth grade championship."

"Were you on the team?" Mark asked.

"Yup," said Craig. "But I didn't really play that much. Mostly I subbed, you know, went in when we were ahead. But this past summer I went to a soccer camp for three weeks, so I think I might get to see more playing time. How 'bout you? Were you on a team?"

"Uh-huh," Mark mumbled. "But not around here."

"Where?"

Mark debated whether he should tell Craig he'd lived in England. If he did, Craig would probably want to know why he had lived there — and why he had moved back. *That* would lead to questions about where he lived now. Mark still wasn't sure if he wanted his future teammates to know that he lived with his grandparents because his parents were getting a divorce.

But one look at Craig's open, honest face made him decide to tell him the truth — about England, anyway.

"The last team I played on was in England," he said.

"England! Wow! I saw them play in the World Cup on TV. They're nuts about soccer, huh?"

Mark grinned, "Yeah, it's really popular over there."

"So you must be a real hotshot player," Craig said.

"I mean, playing in England and having your mother as a coach —"

"I told you, she doesn't coach anymore," Mark interrupted sharply.

Craig looked surprised at the tone of his voice. "Sorry. You did mention that the other day, didn't you?" He looked at Mark curiously but said nothing else.

Mark was embarrassed. How could I snap at the first person who's tried to be friendly? he thought.

"It's just that she's got a career now, so she doesn't have time to coach." Mark fiddled with his locker combination. "Sorry I blew up at you. I guess I'm just nervous because I don't know if the way I played in England will work here." The memory of how he had misread the dark-haired boy's head signal the previous day flashed through his mind.

Craig shrugged. "Guess it doesn't matter," he said. "Soccer is soccer, whether you play it here or in England. Long as you play a good game now, Coach'll put you on the team. That's all that counts, right?"

Mark grinned. Craig was so matter-of-fact. He didn't seem to let anything bother him.

A few of the guys who had been at practice had

overheard the last part of the conversation. They crowded around.

"You played soccer in England?" one of the boys asked. "Cool!"

"Hey, guys, let's keep it under wraps," said another. "We don't want the rest of the league to know we've got a secret weapon!"

"Wait a minute," Mark protested. "It's not like I was in the World Cup. I played for this little school I went to. But they do take it seriously over there, though, and we did have some cool plays. Like there was this one . . ."

Craig and the others crowded around to hear him describe the play. Mark heard himself talking more than he had in weeks. It felt good — and seeing the look of understanding come across his listeners' faces made him realize that even if he messed up on the field, he could at least talk a good game!

That afternoon, practice heated up. The coach put them through their drills faster, and he shouted out directions more rapidly.

"Heads up!"

"Pass that ball!"

"Look around, look around!"

"Defense, get a move on it!"

In between drills, Mark managed to put a few more names with faces. Evan Andrews was another front line hopeful, like Mark, and Johnny Mintz looked able to play a strong midfield position. Both boys were new to the team, too.

Mark also found out who the dark-haired boy was. His name was Vince Loman. He had been the star of the summer league for the past two years and a strong starter for the Scorpions the year before. In fact, the Scorpions had voted him team captain for this year's squad.

He *was* good, Mark noticed. Vince clearly knew how to move the ball into striking range, and his dribbling and passing were controlled and accurate.

I just hope he isn't still holding a grudge against me for my goof-up yesterday, Mark thought.

Mark had his chance to find out before the practice was through. During the first scrimmage, he was paired up with Vince in the forward line. Vince was at center, and Mark was to his left.

No sooner had play started than Vince intercepted a ball obviously meant for Mark. Vince swooped in and captured it with his left foot. Then, after dribbling it for a few yards, he passed it — to his right wing, in the opposite direction from Mark.

Mark's eyes narrowed, but he jogged downfield with the rest of the front line, ready for a pass if one came his way.

Coach Ryan had worked out a few simple plays for them to try in the scrimmage. One called for the forward line to make a rush at the goal while a backfielder swept around and dashed right in front of the goal. With any luck, he would be in position for a short kick across the line and into the net.

When Vince called out the signal for that play, his wings rushed forward. From the corner of his eye, Mark saw the backfielder start his sweep. But an opposing lineman jumped in his way. The backfielder tripped and toppled over.

Mark knew the play couldn't go as planned. So, breaking from his own pattern, he swung around to approach the goal in place of the backfielder.

Meanwhile, Vince had decided to kick the ball for a goal instead of passing it. His boot was high, but weak — an easy pickoff for the goalie, who ran forward to catch it.

Instead, he found himself grasping at air. At the last second, Mark had rushed forward and headed the ball over his shoulder and into the net.

Goal!

Cheers rang out from the guys on the sidelines. It had looked like a brilliant play, well practiced, even though it was just an improvisation on Mark's part.

Mark was all smiles as he ran back down the field. He glanced over at Vince to give him the thumbs-up sign. But Vince had his head down.

"Hey, Captain, great assist!" Mark called out.

Vince's head shot up. "It would have been a goal if you hadn't jumped in to grab the glory," he replied stiffly.

Mark didn't think; he just blurted, "I don't think so. The goalie was going to catch it easily. Your kick was too soft."

Vince glowered and balled his fists. "Is that right? Well, I'll just have to kick harder next time, then, won't I?" He spun on his heels and took up his position in center field.

Mark was stunned. Ever since his playground league days, he'd been taught that a goal was a goal, no matter who made it. But it seemed obvious that Vince thought otherwise.

Or had Mark been wrong in thinking the kick would be caught? Maybe he had acted too hastily — and Vince was angry because he thought Mark was showing off?

Coach Ryan switched players around for the next few plays, and Mark eventually found himself in the center spot. Vince was now playing his left wing. Mark was determined to use the opportunity to set up a play that would put Vince in scoring position. He wanted to show him that there were no hard feelings.

But he never got a chance. Even though his team-mates must have been able to see that Mark knew what he was doing, he didn't seem to be getting his share of the passes. In fact, Mark started to feel like Vince was hogging the ball. Before he could be sure, though, a whistle blew.

"Okay, guys," Coach Ryan called. "That's it for to-day. Tomorrow is our last tryout practice. Then I'll be posting a roster of the starting lineup and the substitutes. Our first game is against the Raiders next Friday, and we need to start working out as a regular team. So do your laps now, do your home-work later, and come prepared tomorrow for an-other hard practice."

As the boys dispersed, Craig came over to Mark and said, "You're a shoo-in for a spot on the team."

"You think so?" Mark asked.

"Definitely. But don't get carried away," he added. "Coach Ryan didn't mention it, but everyone makes the team. Of course, only eleven guys get to start, and there are only five substitutes who suit up each game. But anyone else who wants a shot can con-tinue to practice with the team and come along to games as reserves."

Mark was pleased to hear about Coach Ryan's pol-icy. But he knew he wouldn't be content to be a re-serve. He wanted to be listed as one of the starting eleven.

Two days later, he got his wish. The roster was posted, and his name was way up top, even above Vince Loman's. For some reason, that made him feel great — even when he noticed that the list was in alphabetical order.

4

Soccer and school whizzed by, and before Mark knew it, it was the first game of the season. Friday afternoon was sunny and cold, just the way he liked it for a game.

When he stepped out on to the Knightstown Middle School soccer field in his scarlet shirt and his silver-gray shorts, he was revved up and ready to play ball. Looking over to the grandstand behind the Scorpions' bench, he could see Grandma and Grandpa Conway huddled together. They saw him looking in their direction and waved.

Craig booted a white-and-black sphere in his direction.

"Go, Scorpions!" shouted the freckle-faced red-head.

"Go, yourself, Pepper!" Mark called back. He smiled wide as he kicked the ball back to Craig.

Over the past week and a half, he had grown comfortable with Craig and some of the other guys. In fact, most of his teammates seemed to have accepted him with eagerness. Only Vince Loman kept his distance, and though Mark didn't understand what the boy had against him, he decided to just try to ignore it.

Of course, there had been that bad moment when both boys had called for a different play at the same time. Vince had had possession of the ball, but Mark had better field position to see the way a setup could work. Half the guys had listened to Mark. The other half had listened to Vince. As a result, neither play worked, and the defense had stolen the ball. Vince had frowned at Mark but said nothing.

Later on, though, during a break, Coach Ryan had reminded Mark that only the player with the ball should call for a play. Mark had nodded. He understood the reasoning behind such a rule; the mess-up on the field had shown him its importance clearly.

He thought that was the end of the incident. But Vince saw fit to drum it home every chance he got.

"Think that's the way they play over in England?" Mark overheard Vince ask Charlie Burns. "Man, it must have been mass confusion on the field. Or maybe the loudest voice got to call the shots." Vince glanced at Mark, smirked, then ran onto the field.

Even now, three days later, Mark's face burned at the memory. But he just swallowed it and concentrated on his warm-up drills.

I only hope things go more smoothly today, he thought.

Mark was set to play the middle of the forward line, and Vince would be on his right. They would be a winning combination at scoring if they could get in sync with each other. In a few seconds, Mark would find out.

The Scorpions lined up in a three-three-four format: completing the forward three was veteran lineman Evan Andrews, to Mark's left; Jim Shields, Mel Duffy, and John Mintz, three rookies like Mark, were at midfield; and Craig, Eddie Chu, Harvey Kahn, and Stu Watts manned the backfield. Charlie Burns was the Scorpions' goalie.

Tweeeeet!

The ref blew the whistle, signaling the start of the

game. He placed the ball in the center of the field, and the players took their positions.

The Knightstown Scorpions stood out in their scarlet and gray. The late-day sunshine lit up the Terryville Raiders in their mustard yellow and blue uniforms.

The Scorpions had won the coin toss and elected to kick.

Mark knew what his job would be. He was to fake a pass to Evan Andrews, then quickly shoot the ball to Vince. The team captain would then set up the first play of the game. It was a simple enough thing to do.

But it didn't go as planned. When Mark readied himself to put the ball in play with his first tap, he noticed that the Raiders' defense was lined up more heavily on Vince's side of the field. It was as if they knew the ball was going to end up with Vince and were ready to stop him.

Mark had to make a tough decision. Should he keep to the original play or improvise? As the whistle blew to start the game, Mark checked out the Raiders' lineup one last time.

Then he kicked the ball — to Evan Andrews.

Evan looked surprised, but he recovered fast and dribbled the ball down the field. Mark and Vince raced down their lanes, too, as Evan avoided first one defensive player, then another.

But that was as far as he got. A Raider snagged it away from Evan and booted it in the opposite direction.

Eddie Chu was the first Scorpion to get a piece of it. He tried to kick it into the clear, but a couple of Raiders got in the way. The ball sailed off toward the sideline. Stu Watts trapped it and dribbled it forward until he was besieged by Raiders. He passed the ball toward the midfield, halfway between Mark and Vince.

Both boys charged at it at breakneck speed. But Mark could see that Vince was a little bit ahead of him. He backed off just in time for Vince to capture the ball. With a clear field ahead, the Scorpion wing began to dribble toward the goal.

It wasn't long before he was overtaken by a couple of fast-moving Raiders. Mark could see Vince looking around to see which of his teammates was in the open. Mark was the closest, but Evan Andrews was shouting for the ball, too. Vince twisted around and booted the ball in Evan's direction just seconds before a Raider defensive man attacked.

Evan dribbled the ball for a few feet, then pivoted and booted the ball across the field to Mark.

Mark trapped it, then nudged the ball forward with the inside of his right shoe. But the Raiders' defense was fierce. The Knightstown center held on to the ball for only a few minutes before it was stolen by some fancy footwork on the part of the Raiders' center halfback.

A quick kick by the halfback sent the ball deep into Scorpion territory. The Raiders' left wing swooped in and carried the ball close to the goal. He drew his leg back and kicked the ball toward the net — hard.

But goalie Charlie Burns was ready. He scooped it up and sent it flying back down toward the midfield stripe.

Mark had hung back enough to be in position for the ball when it came his way. A pass from Jim Shields gave him possession. In the distance, he could hear the approach of Raiders defensemen. But he dribbled the ball forward and stayed ahead of them. Out of the corner of his eye, he could see that both Vince and Evan had trailed him down the field and were ready to help out.

Glancing ahead, Mark saw that his way to the goal was blocked. As much as he wanted to be the first on the team to score, he knew it would be smarter to pass the ball to someone who had a better shot. Without hesitation, he booted the ball to Vince. The Scorpion captain trapped the ball, paused, then kicked it toward the net.

The Raiders' goalie leapt up and managed to stop the ball before it crossed the line.

"Nice try," Mark called over to Vince as the ball sailed over their heads. But Vince didn't even glance at him as they reversed direction and started running back downfield.

Mark knew it was possible Vince just hadn't heard him. Somehow, though, he guessed Vince was choosing to ignore him. But why?

He didn't have time to think about it any further. Mel Duffy had stolen the ball from a Raider forward and had just passed it in his direction. Mark stopped it with his right foot and started to move down the field toward the Raiders' goal again. But the field was loaded with Raiders, and there was no clear path. He dribbled the ball, looking for someone to pass to.

A pair of Raiders double-teamed him. One snaked a foot in, stole the ball, and sent it toward his own front line.

Mark pulled up short, then jogged slowly to center field. He glanced over at Vince, who was doing the same. Although the boy didn't look at him, Mark was sure he saw a trace of a smile on Vince's face.

I must have imagined that, Mark thought. Vince can't be glad that something bad happened when I tried to take the ball downfield. Can he?

Suddenly Mark wasn't so sure. Everything that had happened so far between the two boys indicated that Vince might be perfectly content if Mark failed on the field.

The little flicker of anger Mark had felt earlier in the day flamed a little higher at the thought. But as before, he pushed it away and turned his attention back to the game.

Soon enough, the ball came back toward the Raiders' goal. Mark watched Vince bear down on it. Mark had to admit that he was one of the best players on the field. The Scorpions' captain seemed to be everywhere at once. He stole, dribbled, and passed with great accuracy.

Vince's onslaught had exhausted the Raiders' defense. One player tried to boot the ball clear from in front of the goal, but his kick was off. Vince grabbed his chance. With a great leap, he headed the airborne ball toward their net — and in it went for the first goal of the game!

As the crowd cheered, the team crowded around Vince to give him slaps on the back and high fives. Mark joined in, but just as he was about to offer his congratulations, the ref blew the whistle to signal the continuation of the game.

Mark glanced toward the sideline as he started to follow the action down the field. There were Grandma and Grandpa Conway and, squeezed in next to them, his father! It looked as though Mr. Conway was going to find time for him after all.

The ball was now deep in Scorpions territory. Craig and Eddie Chu were bearing down on the Raiders' forwards. There were two quick attempts at a kick on goal. But misfired. Still, the Scorpions just couldn't seem to get the ball out of the circle.

Tweeet!

A penalty was called — against the Scorpions!

Johnny Mintz had gotten so tangled up with a Raiders wing, he had committed a minor foul. The Raiders would get a free kick.

Mark hustled over to the goal line. Coach Ryan used his forward line to form the wall defending the goal area.

The kick was a fireball that Evan Andrews, lined up on Mark's right, somehow managed to block. Jim Shields collected it and dribbled a few yards before passing it on to Mel Duffy. The ball moved steadily downfield, crossing the midfield line. Finally the Scorpions were deep into Raiders territory. Vince took possession.

"Come on, Scorpions!" Mark called as he raced downfield. He was careful to keep at least one defensive man between him and the goal so that he wouldn't be called offsides. But he made sure he was in good position to dart ahead should the ball come his way.

So far, though, Vince had passed to him exactly once — and then it was only because Mark caught up with the ball before it got to its intended receiver. Despite the fact that they had both been constantly moving back and forth, up and down, and across the field as a team, there was almost no contact between them.

But as the play became concentrated in the penalty area, they had to pay more attention to each other. A screw-up here could be costly.

Vince had just wriggled free of two Raiders defensemen. He looked around, then half-dribbled, half-booted the ball toward the center of the circle.

Mark swooped in to trap it. As he lifted his head, it looked as though he would have a good shot on goal. Then a Raider stepped in front of him, leaving the player he had been guarding wide open. That player was Evan. Mark booted it to him.

The Raider jumped back toward Evan, but Evan was too quick. He stopped the ball, then instantly returned it to Mark. The Raider was caught out of position — and Mark took advantage of the opportunity. In one smooth motion, he stopped the ball, bent his knee, and let fly.

The ball zoomed through the air, passed the goalie's outstretched arms, and hit its target.

Goal!

The score was now Scorpions 2, Raiders 0.

This time the team crowded around Mark and Evan, slapping them on their backs and palms. Mark noticed that Vince hovered around the edge of the group and was the first one to leave when the ref blew his whistle to signal the end of the first half.

Evan rushed up to Mark and started to crow about the goal.

"It was a classic!" he said, brushing his sweaty hair back off his brow. "What a combo. Almost like a give-and-go in basketball!"

Mark smiled and nodded. "It's a play we did in England a few times, but I'd forgotten about it until now. It really works when the defense isn't prepared. Plus you can feed the ball to the center position from either side of the field. Maybe Coach Ryan'll add it to our playbook."

Mark heard a snort come from behind him. He turned to see Vince laughing with another teammate. He thought he heard the word "brownnose" come out of Vince's mouth.

Is that what he's got against me? Mark thought. He thinks I'm sucking up to the coach, just because I've got a play to suggest?

Mark found that hard to believe, though. When

he had played in England, his teammates had often worked with the coach to come up with good plays. After all, weren't the players on the field just as knowledgeable about what could and couldn't work as the people standing on the sidelines? Even when his mother had coached, she had sometimes bounced ideas off her players.

The second-half whistle blew, and play resumed. The Scorpions couldn't seem to do anything wrong. Both Vince and Mark scored goals. The home team allowed their opponents one goal in the last few seconds of the game, leaving the final score Scorpions 4, Raiders 1.

The fans loved every minute of it. When the whistle blew to signal the end of the game, they swarmed out of the stands. Cheers and hugs slowed down the team as they made their way toward a table that had been set up with refreshments for the players.

"Great game, son!" Mark's father was the first one to reach him. He gave him a warm embrace.

"Two goals — my, oh, my," said Grandma Conway. "This calls for a party. I'm glad I made something special for dinner. We'll all celebrate together."

But Mr. Conway shook his head. "I won't be able to make it," he said.

"Do you have to work again tonight, Dad?" Mark asked, disappointed.

Mr. Conway's face darkened. "No, I have to meet my lawyer," he said angrily. "Your mother just won't let up on her demands. Why, she thinks she can —"

"Bill," Grandma Conway interrupted quietly. She shook her head.

Mr. Conway looked at her, then glanced at Mark. "Well, anyway, I guess I'd better get going." He gave Mark a fleeting kiss on the cheek and rushed off.

"Oh, look at these lovely cookies," said Grandma Conway. "You'd better not eat too many and spoil your dinner."

Mark stared at the ground. "I'm not very hungry. Come on," he said to Craig, who had been standing with him the whole time. "We'd better get cleaned up."

As they got inside the locker room, Craig asked, "What was that all about?"

"Nothing," said Mark.

"Nothing, huh?" said Craig. "Well, I guess it's nothing you'd want to even tell a friend about."

Mark twisted his towel into a knot and looked at the friendly face staring at him.

"It's not that," he said. "It's — it's — it's just, well, you see, I'm not living where I used to because I'm not living with my parents anymore."

Craig cocked his head and asked, "You're not? Why? I mean, why not?"

"Because they're not living together because they're getting a divorce." He realized it was the first time he had said it out loud. He went on, "And they both want me to live with them, and all they do is fight over it. So I'm living with my grandparents. It's no big deal."

"If you say so, Mark," Craig said quietly, his usual joking manner subdued, "then it's no big deal. No sweat."

47

5

Mrs. Conway steered the dark green convertible into a parking space close to the main entrance to the mall. Mark unbuckled his seat belt and got out.

"I really don't need anything," he said for what seemed like the hundredth time that day. He pushed his way through the revolving door behind her.

"Of course you do," she insisted, taking his arm and steering him toward the mall's biggest department store. "In a store this large, you're sure to find something you want. Besides, how do I know you have all your school clothes? As a matter of fact, do you have enough underwear and socks?"

That made Mark smile.

"I should have enough socks. You send them to me from all over the world!" He bit back the rest of what he was thinking: that it would be nicer for him to receive more than the short note she stuck in with each pair. He didn't want to ruin her good mood by sounding mean-spirited.

Mrs. Conway laughed. "Just be glad I stopped sending underwear! Remember that pair I sent you with the little bears hugging and kissing?"

"Yuck! I'll never forget the time they were the only pair I had that weren't in the laundry. And that was the day we had gym class!" Mark said. "Boy, did I ever take a pounding from the rest of the guys."

"Oh, I can't believe those English boys had never seen anything like that," said Mrs. Conway.

"Don't kid yourself," said Mark. "Those English kids could be tough. You never really got to know them."

As soon as the words were out of his mouth, he was sorry he'd spoken them. He never said things like that to his parents. After all, it didn't help matters.

They had reached the Boys' Department. Rows and rows of neatly buttoned shirts hung on racks like a regiment of well-trained soldiers. Tables stacked with creased and folded trousers were aligned according to size and color. At Mark's comment, Mrs.

Conway put down the blue-and-white-striped rugby shirt she was examining and put her hands on his shoulders.

"I tried to," she said. "I simply didn't have the time. I guess you just didn't get the kind of 'milk and cookies' mom you wanted."

"I didn't mean that," Mark mumbled. "Forget I said anything."

The two wandered silently between the rows of clothing. Then Mark saw the sporting goods section.

"Hey, do you think they sell soccer shoes here?"

"Why? Do you need a pair?" asked his mother.

"Well, you're the one who taught me that a good-fitting sport shoe is important if you're going to play well. And my old pair is starting to feel a little tight," Mark replied.

"Well, then, let's see about getting you the best pair of soccer shoes they have. Excuse me," she said to the salesperson. "Do you have soccer shoes?"

The woman pointed the way. A few minutes later, they were surrounded by fishing rods, skis, tennis racquets, and sleeping bags. Mark spotted a display with a big basket of black-and-white soccer balls.

"Gotta be nearby," he said. "Oh, there they are." He pointed to a wall with boxes and boxes of all kinds of sporting footwear — baseball cleats, running shoes, basketball high-tops, and over on one side, soccer shoes.

Mrs. Conway checked her watch, then handed him her credit card.

"Just find the ones you want, try them on, and if they fit and you like them, pay for them with this. Just tell the salesperson I'll be back to sign for them," she said.

"Where are you going?" he asked.

"There's a pay phone over on that wall. I have to call into my office."

"But this is Saturday," Mark protested.

"Sorry, sweetie," she said. She paused a moment, then went on in a hushed voice, "I didn't want to tell you this until I knew something more definite, but maybe it's better you know what's happening now. Mark, it seems that my company might be moving out of state sometime soon. I'm hoping I will be moving with them — and if the court decides you're to stay with me, you'll be coming with me."

51

Mark's heart sank. Moving again? he thought.

But out loud, all he said was, "I guess that's why you don't have time for soccer right now."

"Oh, Mark, I'll try to get to some of your games," she said. "It's just that afternoons are so hard."

"Yeah, but you used to have time. Some of the guys on the team even remember when you coached us all those years ago."

"They do? That was fun, wasn't it?" Mrs. Conway got a faraway look in her eyes. But then that look changed. "Well, that was then. Now, thanks to your father, I simply don't have the luxury of doing such things. Every spare minute I have, I have to spend with my lawyers." She straightened up and started for the phone. "I won't be a minute. You just go and get your shoes. Get good ones, too."

Mark sighed deeply. He wished he'd never brought up the subject of coaching, or soccer, or how things used to be. It just didn't do any good.

He turned toward the display of soccer shoes. None of them looked any good to him now. He wasn't even sure he wanted a new pair.

"May I help you?" A salesman stepped out from behind the counter.

"I don't think so," said Mark.

"We're having a special sale on these top-of-the-line soccer shoes," he said, pointing at a famous brand. "I might have something in your size."

Mark hesitated. "Well, maybe I could just try them on," he said, nodding to the salesman.

A few minutes later, Mark was carrying a bag with his new soccer shoes and looking for his mother. But the floor was too crowded now for him to see all the way over to the telephone booths.

"Hey, Mark, what's happening?" called a familiar voice.

Mark turned around and saw Craig Crandall. Eddie Chu and Mel Duffy were standing with him over by the soccer ball display.

"Nothing," Mark replied automatically. Then he added, "What are you guys doing here? Buying a new soccer ball?"

"No, Mel got one here last week and it had a leak. So we brought it back to exchange it for a good one," said Eddie. "We're just about ready to go and get some pizza for lunch. How about you?"

"Oh, I just got here. My mom drove me over. She's making a phone call," Mark said.

53

"Whadja buy?" asked Mel.

As Mark was showing them his new soccer shoes, his mother returned. Mark introduced Craig, Eddie, and Mel. His mother smiled at each boy, but her eye lingered on Craig for a minute.

"I know you! You used to play on my soccer team way back when!" she said. "Pepper!"

Craig nodded and opened his mouth to reply. But Mark, afraid that Craig might bring up the past and set his mother off, as he himself had done earlier, cut him off.

"These guys are going to have pizza, Mom, so I guess we'd better let them head out."

"Can't Mark come with us, Mrs. Conway?" Craig asked.

"Of course he can," she said. "I'll sign for those shoes. Then I have some shopping of my own to do, and we can meet up later on. Mark," she called as he moved away with his friends, "before you go, may I have my credit card back?"

She took the card and slipped a large bill into Mark's hand. "That's for the pizza. Treat your friends. I don't want the change."

"Come on," Eddie Chu called. "Some of the other guys are going to meet us there."

Mark watched his mother walk away, then stuffed the bill in his pocket and joined the others. With Mark toting his new shoes and Mel holding his replacement ball under his arm, they made tracks for the pizzeria. By the time they got there, Jim Shields and Charlie Burns were already seated at a big table in the corner.

"'Bout time," said Charlie. "We had trouble holding this table. Hey, Mark, you gonna eat with us? Do they eat pizza over in England?"

"Uh-huh," Mark said, "to both questions!"

"We'd better get another chair over here, then," said Jim.

"Why? There are six of us, six chairs," said Eddie.

"Vince said he was coming, too," answered Jim.

Mark stiffened. He wasn't sure how he felt about spending time with Vince off the soccer field.

But before he had a chance to come up with a reason for leaving, Vince arrived. "Pizza's on me, guys," he said grandly as he slid into his seat. He slapped a bill on the table and grinned. "There's enough for three six-slicers if we get just cheese only. Three slices apiece should be plenty, I'd say."

"But there are seven of us," Craig said. He sat back and pointed at Mark, whom he had been blocking from Vince's view.

Vince's eyes narrowed. "Well, that's all the money I have, so someone's going to have to survive with less."

Mark fumbled in his pocket for the money his mother had given him. It was more than Vince had laid on the table.

"Well, why don't we just pay for it with this instead and get whatever we want?" he said.

"Cool!" said Craig, reaching for Mark's money.

Vince stared at Mark. "What makes his money better than mine?" he asked with a hard edge to his voice.

The other boys exchanged glances. It seemed they were suddenly aware that something was wrong.

Craig was the first one to break the stony silence. "Hey, I've got an idea. Vince, since you're so keen on spending your money, why don't you get us some sodas now and then some ice cream after the pizza? Speaking for myself, I'm more than happy to let both of you treat me to as much food as your money will buy!"

The other boys all laughed, and eventually Mark, and then Vince, joined in. But even so, the pizza party wasn't the fun time Mark had originally hoped it would be.

6

The next day at school, Craig cornered Mark at his locker.

"Okay, what gives?"

Craig didn't have to elaborate. Mark knew that he was asking about what had happened between him and Vince at the pizza parlor.

"I don't know. Maybe you can tell me why our team captain is holding a grudge against me," Mark replied.

But Craig couldn't shed any light on the subject. In fact, he tried to tell Mark that Vince's behavior had been out of the ordinary. Even when Mark recounted some of Vince's on-field slights, Craig shook his head in disbelief.

"It would be dumb for Vince not to want to make his team's forward line as strong and wily as possible," he reasoned. "So you must be imagining it. But if you really believe it," he added, "then you should just corner Vince and tell him how you feel about it!"

Despite Craig's assurances, Mark was unconvinced. To his mind, he and Vince were enemies and yesterday's scene had just proven that Vince felt the same way. And he was sure that talking to Vince about it would do no good.

In the meantime, he was determined to continue ignoring it on the soccer field. School was okay and he was glad he had made some good friends, but soccer was the most important thing to him right now. He wasn't about to let anything interfere with his playing.

His determination showed during practice. More and more he was becoming an important part of the team. It was obvious that he and Vince were the real standouts in the Scorpions' lineup.

Mark had learned that Vince was not only team captain but had been voted Most Valuable Player last year as well. And when Mark put his personal feelings aside, he had to admit that Vince deserved the title. He was a real scientist when it came to offensive maneuvers. Slick dribbling, head fakes, body swerves, and speed — he had them all and used them time and again to set up goal attempts.

But Mark was his equal in all those things — and one more. Mark could keep his head in difficult situations. Vince would flare up and lose control when things weren't going smoothly. But Mark stayed calm under pressure.

Some of the guys had starting calling Mark "Mr. Inside" and Vince "Mr. Outside" because of their field positions at center and wing — apparently not realizing that the names had a second meaning as well.

Practice that afternoon ended in a scrimmage, as always.

"Nice work, you guys," Coach Ryan called from the sideline. He blew the whistle to end the scrimmage. Twenty-two sweaty, tired players trotted off the field to join him at the bench.

As they toweled off some of the sweat, the coach beckoned to Mark. "See anything out there that would fool the English?" he said half-jokingly. Over the past few weeks, Mark had given the coach a few suggestions for plays based on what he had learned in England. The coach had tried a few of them; others he had said were too complex for the Scorpions squad right now. Mark disagreed but knew better than to argue.

Now he said, "Well, the team I was on in England played an incredible offensive game. We had a strong front line; we worked together like a well-oiled machine, you know?"

The coach looked at him for a moment, then said, "I hope our front line will be as strong before the season's out." Mark blushed, not sure if the coach was suggesting that Mark could play better — or if he was referring to something else. Could it be he had noticed the lack of camaraderie between Vince and Mark and was asking Mark to bury the hatchet for the good of the team?

The coach turned to the rest of the players and talked about the upcoming game against the Concord Tigers. The Tigers were new in the league, and not much was known about them.

"Okay, we'll stick with our three-three-four line-up, with the usual starters, until we see what we're up against. Now, just do your laps and get out of here. I want you all rested up and in good shape for these Tigers. We'll show 'em how we play ball in Knightstown, right?"

"Go, Scorpions!"

"Team! Team! Scorpions!"

The shouts rang out as the players all rushed off the bench to bear down on the dirt track surrounding the soccer field.

That evening, Mark could hardly sleep. He kept wondering about the coach's comment.

Maybe I have been just as much at fault as Vince, he thought. Maybe all it'll take is for me to put out my hand for him to shake.

He rolled over to a more comfortable position.

Then again, he thought, knowing Vince, he'll just look at it and laugh. Or worse, sneer and accuse me of kissing up to the captain. No, he decided finally, it'd be better to just leave the situation alone. I can deal with it. The Scorpions are doing okay with the way things are. Who am I to say that they could be better?

7

I'm giving you an extra-big apple to have with lunch," Grandma Conway said to Mark at breakfast. "For good luck — and extra energy."

"An apple for good luck?" Grandpa Conway scratched his head. "That's a new one on me."

"Oh, hush up, you," she said. "You just make sure you get back here in time to pick me up for the game. We want to get good seats."

"I'll eat the whole apple, Grandma," Mark promised with a smile. "Don't you worry. And I'm sure there'll be plenty of good seats left. Probably too many."

As soon as the words left his mouth, he was sorry. He didn't want his grandparents to think that he cared about whether his father — or his mother — showed up. In fact, the very thought of the two of them both showing up at the same game sent a chill down his spine. The crowd was never so big that they wouldn't see each other. And then one of them would be sure to say something. And the other would answer back. The next thing you knew, they'd be fighting and he'd be caught in the middle. Again.

"Rats. I'm on the bench this time." Craig stared at the game roster Coach Ryan had posted in the locker room as he did for every game. "But it looks like the coach is sticking with you and Vince in the front line."

"Hey, the way Coach Ryan sends in subs, you'll see some action, I'm sure," said Mark.

It was true. The coach tried to give as many of the players as possible some time on the field. But he was smart enough to stick with his winners, too.

The Concord Tigers took to the field in their black-and-orange-striped jerseys and orange shorts. In terms of size, they didn't look all that different from the Knightstown kids. Watching them from the corner of his eye during the warm-up periods, Mark could see that they were revved up for the game, too.

When the two teams ran out into position for the kickoff, Vince jogged by Mark. Neither boy said a word, but Vince's hazel eyes burned into Mark's for a brief moment.

Then the ref placed the ball in the center circle, stepped back, and blew the whistle.

The Scorpions had won the toss and chosen to kick. Mark hooked his foot under the ball and sent it in a low, fast arc to Evan Andrews. Evan quickly kicked it to Johnny Mintz, who had sped by him near the outside line. Then Evan took off, running directly ahead of Johnny, and Johnny returned the ball to him. It was a classic "through pass" maneuver that had worked well in practice — and worked now, too. The Scorpions were deep into Tiger territory.

Evan dribbled the ball for a moment, then passed it to Mark. Mark wasted no time moving it across the field to Vince. The Scorpion right wing had the ball for only a second before two Tiger midfielders charged him. He tried to get rid of it, but his kick was blocked.

With possession of the ball, the Tigers wasted no time moving it in the opposite direction. They crossed the halfway line into Scorpion territory for the first time. With the advantage of a little speed and some smart passing, they faced a clear field on their way toward the goal area.

But the Scorpions got a break. An overeager Tiger booted the ball toward a receiver too fast, and it went sailing out of bounds. Since it was on his side of the field, Vince went for the throw-in.

Mark knew the ball would not come his way. It wasn't just because Vince so rarely included him in his plays: Coach Ryan designed such throw-ins to be received by his midfielders, so that his front line could get in position to move the ball up the field. So Mark got set to assist whichever teammate ended up with the ball.

In this case, it turned out to be Mel Duffy, who caught it between his knees. The ball dropped to the ground, and Mel looked around to see who was in the clear. Mark waved and shouted, and Mel found him. A short pass in his direction gave the Scorpions' center forward all he needed to break away down the field toward the defenders' goal.

Feeling the heat of a couple of oncoming Tiger tacklers, Mark spied Vince heading for the exact spot he needed to be in for a goal attempt. A quick stop and a well-placed kick in Vince's direction, and the Scorpion wing had all he needed. Vince booted the ball toward the left corner of the net.

It was good!

The Scorpions had drawn "first blood" and were on the scoreboard, 1–0.

The fans in the bleachers exploded with cheers. Mark could see his grandparents waving their arms in the air and yelling with the rest. But he didn't see anyone else sitting with them.

Despite the early goal, it was soon apparent that the Tigers were just warming up. In the next few minutes of play, they were all over the Scorpions. Vince called out to his team, "Come on, you guys, look around!" Mark, too, tried to jolt the other guys with shouts of encouragement whenever he saw something good happening.

"Nice trap, Eddie!"

"Way to go, Mel!"

But there was no stopping the Tigers from getting on the scoreboard. Midway through the first half, they scored their first goal to tie the game at 1–1. Even worse, they were controlling the ball so well, it looked like they were going to go ahead any second.

Charlie Burns had made three spectacular saves. Each looked tougher than the one before it.

"Hang in there, Charlie!" Coach Ryan called from the sidelines. "Give him some help, you guys! Dig in!"

And from the stands came the loud repeated sound of "De-*fense!* De-*fense!*"

Mark stayed in his own zone, pitching in on defense whenever he could. But he kept himself ready to move the ball toward the Tigers' goal if he got the chance.

His opening came in the final seconds of the first half. The Scorpions had defended successfully against four goal attempts. By now, even the dogged Tigers were playing a little sloppy.

First, Harvey Kahn got into a snarl with a Tiger forward and caused the ball to squirt within Mel Duffy's reach. Mel trapped it with the inside of his left foot, then booted it with his right over to Jim Shields. Jim zigged it across the field to Mark, who was all by himself — not a Tiger in sight.

The Scorpions' center forward dribbled the ball straight down the field. But within seconds he began to hear the oncoming thud of defensemen bearing down on him. When they were practically on top of him, Mark pointed and waved to his left — but with his left foot, he booted the ball over to Vince on his right. Since all the attention was focused the other way for a split second, Vince had a clear shot at the goal. He lined up and kicked the ball forward.

Goal!

The Scorpions had practiced that play only once during the previous week. Yet it worked like clockwork. Mark was proud that he had been able to carry it off. He looked over at Vince to give him a thumbs-up sign, but Vince had already headed back to the forward line.

"Heckuva play, you guys!" Mark shouted out anyhow. Then he moved into position. At the whistle, he nudged the ball over to Johnny Mintz. The ball came right back at him, but there wasn't enough time left in the half to do much more than let the clock run out.

"Yes!" said Craig, leaping up from the bench as Mark came off the field.

The Scorpions' center forward chugged a large drink of water. Then he wiped off his forehead and flopped down in front of the coach — but not before glancing into the stands. There were his grand-parents, smack behind the bench. Just behind them, he saw his father, all smiles, leaning over and point-ing toward the Scorpions. Mark was about to shift his eyes back to the coach when he spotted someone else he knew.

Off to one side of the stands, huddled up and drinking from a paper coffee cup, was his mother. She was smiling, too, and talking to a woman seated next to her. The woman had bright red hair, a lot like Craig's. Mark guessed that it must be his mother.

Mark's heart sank. Just what I don't need, he thought, Mom and Dad at the same game. At least they're not seated together. Still, they're within shout-ing distance. Oh, gosh, I hope that doesn't start up! Everyone will know in a minute who they are and that I'm —

"Mark, are you still with us?" the coach asked, in-terrupting his thoughts.

Mark realized he hadn't heard a word that Coach Ryan had been saying.

"Uh, yes, sir," he mumbled.

The coach looked at him for a long moment, then addressed the team in general. "Okay, then, let's keep our cool out there. Just do what you've learned in practice. I want to see some heads-up ball."

As the Scorpions prepared to take to the field for the second half, Mark noticed that Craig was going in as part of the backfield lineup. He flashed his friend a broad smile.

But that smile faded quickly. From the stands came a sound he had been dreading hearing.

"What do you mean, you're taking Mark out tonight!" Mr. Conway's voice sounded angry. "His grandparents and I have planned a special family dinner together!"

"Well, I've already accepted an invitation for Mark and me, to have dinner with Mark's best friend, Craig, and his mother," Mrs. Conway replied venomously. "Do you even know who Craig is?"

Mark couldn't help but notice the sidelong glances his teammates were giving him. His face turned red, and his stomach burned as if he had swallowed a hot stone. He quickly ducked his head, pretending to tie his shoelaces.

He felt a tap on the shoulder and whirled around. Craig was standing there, an openly concerned look on his face.

"Hey, listen —" he started to say. But Mark cut him off.

"It's nothing," he muttered. "Let's just go play some soccer, okay?"

The Tigers had possession of the ball at the start of the second half. They moved into Scorpion territory quickly, attempting a goal within the first two minutes. But Charlie Burns was on his toes. The Scorpions' goalie sent the ball almost to the center circle, where Johnny Mintz trapped it. But there were too many Tigers surrounding him, and he immediately passed it off to Mark. Mark dribbled it across the halfway line and into Tigers territory.

It didn't take long for an invasion of defenders to close in on him. He passed the ball to Vince. But a Tiger tackler got to it at the same time, and a struggle for possession began. As another Tiger moved in, Mark did the same. The four players twined their legs around the ball until it jiggled free.

Vince and Mark were the closest to the ball as it skidded through the grass. The two of them scrambled toward it at the same speed. But Mark got there just a little ahead of Vince. He thrust his foot forward to take in the ball.

Wham!

A jolt on his hip sent him sprawling.

At first, he thought a Tiger defenseman had snuck up on him. But when the stars in his head cleared, he saw Vince dribbling the ball away in the direction of the Tigers' goal.

Vince knocked me over to get the ball? Mark thought incredulously. But he had to believe what his eyes were showing him. Except for Vince, no one else had been around him. There was no other conclusion to make: Vince had stolen the ball from him!

8

Mark stood up and dusted off his uniform. His leg was smarting where he had fallen on it. But he barely noticed the pain.

"Are you okay?" Coach Ryan called from the sidelines. Mark waved to him to show he was all right and jogged down the field to catch up with the action.

But he wasn't okay. Something had happened to him the minute he saw Vince with the ball. As the throbbing in his leg faded, his blood seemed to boil throughout the rest of his body.

Mark was angrier than he had ever been in his life.

If he wants to play an "every man for himself" game, he thought, then so be it. I've tried to make this front line work, but I can't do it alone. So I'll play it Vince's way from now on.

And with that he threw himself into the play with a savageness he'd never shown before. When the Scorpions had possession of the ball and were moving it toward the Tiger goal, he charged into every play like a wild animal. Twice he committed fouls that cost the Scorpions free kicks. Luckily neither of them went in for a goal.

When the Tigers were attacking the Scorpions' goal, he didn't wait for the defense to clear the ball to him. Instead, he launched himself into the center of the play, often crashing into his own teammates in his rush to get hold of the ball for himself.

In the final moments of the game, Mark threw an elbow at a Tiger wing right in front of the Scorpions' goal. The ref caught the foul and called a penalty kick.

The Scorpions retreated the required ten yards outside the penalty area. Charlie Burns hopped from foot to foot, getting ready for the Tiger wing to take his best shot. A goal now would tie the game.

As Mark watched the ref place the ball on the penalty mark, he realized that this situation was his fault. If he had been playing his usual position, the game might be over now and the Scorpions walking off the field with another win under their belts.

Instead, he was holding his breath, waiting for the ref to blow his whistle, giving the Tiger wing the go-ahead.

Man, what a stupid move, Mark thought. What was I thinking, playing like that?

"Nice going, hotshot," a voice behind him whispered mockingly.

Mark jerked around. Vince, his hands on his knees, was glaring at him.

All the fury Mark had felt earlier came rushing back to him. The ref's whistle blew just as Mark was about to take a step toward Vince.

Mark's eyes followed the ball as it shot toward the goal. Charlie Burns leapt up, arms outstretched — and deflected the ball up and over the net!

A moment later the clock ran out, and the Scorpions jogged off the field amid cheers from the stands.

But Mark didn't feel like celebrating. His mind was a jumble of angry frustration. And when he caught a glimpse of his parents, arguing as they left the bleachers, and of his grandparents' faces twisted with concern, he knew he couldn't take any more. He turned and ran from the field as quickly as he could.

The next morning, Mark picked at his breakfast in stony silence. Food just didn't interest him these days — even the fancy dishes served at the restaurant where he'd gone with Craig and their mothers after the game. He could tell his mother had been disappointed, but he just couldn't help it.

And, on top of that, his leg had a nasty bruise where he had fallen on it the day before. When it was time to go, he slammed the back door and stomped down the driveway to catch the bus. He could feel his grandmother watching him, but he didn't turn around.

At school, his silence continued. He spoke only when asked a question by one of his teachers. And at soccer practice, he played with a ferocity he'd never shown before.

From now on, he said to himself, nobody's going to get near me out on this field. Nobody.

And no one did during practice all week.

Coach Ryan seemed impressed by Mark's intense playing — at first. But on Thursday, he took Mark aside.

"Listen, I know the idea is to get the ball," he said. "But not if that means wrestling your own team-mates for it. Back off a little, and watch for the op-portunities. Remember, you are part of a team, not flying solo."

Mark's scrimmage rotation had just finished. A new group of eleven guys took the field. Mark sat on the bench, watching the action on the field.

"Hey, Mr. Inside, mind a little company, or would you prefer to plot your next strategy?" Craig flopped down next to Mark.

"What do you mean?" Mark asked.

"You're playing every second out there like it's your last. Like you have to control the ball as much as possible," Craig replied.

"Maybe I do," Mark said.

"Okay, my turn," Craig said. "What do *you* mean?"

"I mean it's time I stopped letting certain people walk all over me. It's time I looked out for myself out there. I'm playing to win."

Craig was silent for a moment. Then he crumpled

up his paper cup, stood up, and said quietly, "You ever shake up a bottle of soda, then screw the cap off? That's what you remind me of these days, Mark. Except your cap is still on tight." He dumped the cup in the trash can and walked away.

When he arrived home that night, Mark sat on the edge of his bed and stared down at the floor. His cleats were covered with mud. His shins showed the beginnings of new bruises and scrapes caused by his own aggressive playing that afternoon. His muscles ached.

He pried his shoes off his feet and let them fall to the floor with a thump.

"You okay in there?" came his grandfather's voice from outside his door. "Your dad called a little while ago. Both he and your mother have been trying to get ahold of you all week. They say you haven't been returning their calls. Mark?"

Mark stayed silent. He just didn't feel like talking right now. Not about the game. Not about Vince. And most of all, not about his parents.

9

The next day, Mark kept to himself as much as possible. Still, he couldn't completely avoid Craig. It seemed as though Craig was determined to forget their last conversation. But Mark couldn't.

Craig wouldn't let up. That afternoon, when the Scorpions traveled to Dade City to play the Slickers, Craig slid into the seat next to Mark as always.

"'City Slickers,' get it?" he said.

"Yeah, I get it," said Mark.

"So how come you're not laughing?" Craig asked.

Mark looked at him quickly. But Craig was just smiling his big puppy-dog smile at him. For some reason, that broke through Mark's guard as nothing else could have.

He grinned back. "Is it my fault if your jokes are so lame they fall flat on their faces?" he said. Both boys laughed, and Mark felt better than he had in days.

But the minute the teams took the field for the start of the game, Mark turned serious. Although Coach Ryan's warning echoed through his brain, he wondered if he would be able to play the cool-headed game he usually played — or if the mere sight of Vince would send him into a frenzied tail-spin. He found out soon enough.

The Slickers kicked off and kept control of the ball by crashing through the Scorpions' forward line. They moved the ball all the way into the corner, where a hard-fought struggle for possession took place between Craig and a Slicker wing. The ball bounced free toward Vince. Vince took it on his chest and let it drop in front of him. Then he began to dribble downfield.

He didn't even look up to see if I was open, Mark fumed. But even as the thought crossed his mind, he felt a Slicker defenseman breathing down his neck. He realized it was just as well that Vince hadn't passed off. That Slicker would undoubtedly have been able to swoop in for a steal.

By the time Vince had brought the ball in front of

the Slicker goal, Mark had shaken the defenseman. He was in perfect position for a pass that could result in a goal. But Vince still had possession of the ball. He was the only one who could call the play. And Mark could see that Vince wasn't about to give up the ball so easily.

For a moment, it looked as though Vince was going to have a good shot on the goal. He had expertly evaded his defenseman and was pulling his leg back for a mighty kick. Then quick as a wink, a second Slicker backfielder leapt in front of him and stole the ball.

"Come on, you Scorpions!" Mark shouted as play turned in the other direction.

The Slickers carried the ball into the Scorpions' midfield — but that was as far as they got. Eddie Chu caught up to the ball on a bad pass from one Slicker to another. He wasted no time in booting it directly to Mark.

"Scatter!" Mark yelled as he crossed into Slicker territory.

This play called for the wings and midfielders nearest the sidelines to switch positions. The idea was to confuse the defense long enough to set up a goal attempt. Sometimes it worked. This time the play never got off the ground.

There were a few more hard-fought attempts by the Scorpions to take back control, but the Slickers held out. The play shifted from one side of the field to the other. At one point, Mark made a move toward a ball that had rolled loose in his direction. Three Slickers were all over him instantly.

He shot the ball over to Mel Duffy, who zipped it up to Vince. But the Slicker defense was just too strong. Vince tried to pass it off, but a Slicker wing took the ball away. A few smart moves by that same wing brought him within scoring range.

Moments later, the ball zoomed into the net for the game's first goal. Slickers 1, Scorpions 0.

Charlie Burns banged his fists on his knees. Mark knew the veteran goalie hated to miss the ball. Judging by what he'd seen, Charlie would never have had a chance to stop it. The Slickers were just too good at finding holes in the Scorpions' defense.

And their defense is having no trouble stealing it away from our offense, Mark thought dismally.

Neither side scored again that half, but the Slickers threatened more times than Mark liked to count.

During the halftime break, it was obvious that Coach Ryan was upset with the way his team was playing.

"What's going on out there?" he asked. "Have you all forgotten how to pass the ball? Call for plays? Are you trying to play one-on-eleven? Let me tell you, it doesn't work that way! We're very lucky that scoreboard shows only one goal for their side." He paused to look each of them in the eye.

"Okay," he said finally. "You don't need me to yammer at you like this. You're a skilled team. You just need to use one another more efficiently. Work the plays, and keep the ball moving in the right direction. I want to see Charlie Burns so bored that he's yawning." That brought a smile to the boys' grim faces. As always, Coach Ryan pointed out what was wrong with their playing but never made them feel it was too late to correct it. When the ref's whistle blew to signal the start of the second half, it was a fired-up Scorpions team that took the field.

From the moment play started, it was apparent that the coach's words had struck home. They moved the ball much more quickly. In their very first attack, clean passes flew between all three members of the forward line — Evan Andrews to Mark to Vince and back again. Gradually they brought the ball into firing range of the Slickers' goal.

After breaking away from a couple of Slicker tacklers, Mark saw a chance to set up a play the team had practiced over and over again. He called out, "Scorpion Red!" and faked to the left. Then, planting his left foot firmly on the ground, he booted the ball over to Evan, on his left side. Evan got set right away and kicked the ball high into the air toward the goal. The ball rose over the heads of the blocking Slickers and began to drop in front of the goal. The Slicker goalie positioned himself for the catch.

That's when Mark came zooming behind the blockers. With a powerful leap, he headed the ball into the corner of the net.

Goal!

The scoreboard now read Slickers 1, Scorpions 1.

Groups of Scorpions gathered around Mark and Evan to congratulate them on pulling off the play. Mark was all smiles.

"That worked great!" he exclaimed as he slapped Evan's hand in a high five. "But hey, next time, why don't you swoop in right after me, just in case their goalie blocks me out? If there are two of us right there, one should be able to get control of the ball, right?" Evan looked thoughtful, then nodded in agreement and trotted back to his position.

Mark felt great — until he heard Vince mutter something to Eddie Chu that sounded like "*Oink, oink,* Mr. Know-It-All."

Mark was stunned. Did Vince think he had been hogging the ball? But it had been their cooperative effort that had moved the ball into position! It was just dumb luck that Mark had been the one to call the play.

And what does he mean by calling me Mr. Know-It-All? he thought angrily.

By now it was midway through the second half of the game. Both teams still had a lot of energy and were calling encouragement to their teammates. Try as he might to shake loose of his anger, every time Mark heard Vince's voice among the others, his hackles rose.

His irritation started to show up in his playing. He was so determined to prove he wasn't a ball hog that he overdid it. When a pass came to him, he moved it too quickly to someone else, often catching that person off guard. Once he tripped over the ball because he tried to get rid of it before he had control.

Up until then, Mark had been the most reliable member of the team. Everyone counted on him to be where he was supposed to be. Now he was hanging back, trying to let others have a chance. Confused, the rest of the Scorpions started to misread his intentions. Chances for another goal by the Scorpions began to grow dim.

Then the Knightstown team got a lucky break. A Slicker halfback made a mistake and passed the ball in the wrong direction. It landed smack in the perfect spot for a goal attempt by the Scorpions. Evan Andrews was right there and went for it.

But the Slicker goalie caught the ball and sent it flying back into the middle of the field.

Mark had moved toward center field when he saw Dick making the kick. So when the goalie returned the ball, Mark was in a good position to capture it. But instead, he stood frozen, uncertain if he should move toward it. At the last moment, he decided to go for it.

Unfortunately Eddie Chu had begun to move forward as well. It was too late for Eddie to put on the brakes. He and Mark collided, and the ball bounced right by them both.

The impact sent Mark sprawling to the ground, dazed for a moment. He lay there staring up at the sky.

The referee blew his whistle. Play stopped as Coach Ryan ran onto the field. By the time he reached Mark, Eddie Chu had helped him to his feet. Mark shook his head to try to get rid of the woozy feeling that had come over him. He felt fine a moment later and was relieved to see that Eddie looked no worse for the wear, either.

But Coach Ryan decided Mark could use some time on the bench anyhow. Willie Stubbs came in as Mark left the field.

Mark had been taken out of games before. But usually it was because his team was ahead and the coach wanted to give the substitutes a chance to get in some playing time. But this game was close, and the team they were playing was their toughest competition yet. Mark knew Coach Ryan had replaced him because he wasn't playing his best.

It's all because of Vince, he fumed. If Vince hadn't made that crack, I'd still be in the game. And what did he mean by that, anyway? I was just trying to help Evan see how a good play could be made even better — for the good of the team, for Pete's sake!

Mark was so busy with his thoughts he hadn't realized the game had restarted. With the score tied 1–1 and only minutes remaining in the game, Willie Stubbs sprained his ankle. Coach Ryan had no choice but to ask the ref's permission to send Mark back into the game.

The Scorpions reacted well to his return. Many of the plays depended on a strong center forward, and although Willie was a fine substitute, his skills didn't match Mark's. And since Mark had had some time to cool down — both physically and mentally — he was ready to step back into his role and help his team to victory.

But it didn't look like a victory was going to happen. The Slickers had the ball and were passing it in circles around the defending Scorpions. They came closer and closer to setting up a goal attempt.

And then Harvey Kahn blocked a Slicker wing's pass to another player. The ball slammed into his kneecap and ricocheted across the field at a weird angle. Evan Andrews caught it with his right leg.

He dribbled it across the midfield line. Then he passed it up to Mark.

At first, Mark thought he was in the clear and could take a shot at the goal. But there were just too many players from both teams in his way. Then, out of the corner of his eye, he saw a Scorpion streaking downfield with no one else near him.

It was Craig. Somehow or other, the redheaded backfielder had just dropped out of the picture, and no one was covering him.

Mark protected the ball long enough for Craig to get into position. Then he booted it to him.

Craig controlled it and aimed a kick toward the goal.

It just cleared the underside of the crossbar and sailed into the net.

Goal!

The Scorpions went ahead on the scoreboard and, with only seconds left, closed out the game with a win.

When the Scorpions came off the field, Craig drifted over to the end of the bench, where Mark was knocking the mud off of his soccer shoes.

"Are you okay?" he asked.

"I'm fine," Mark said, surprised.

"You sure didn't look it earlier," said Craig. "Half the time you were all over the ball. The other half, you wouldn't get near it! Were you trying out a new strategy to confuse the defense or something? Because if you were, you should have let the rest of us in on it!"

Even though Mark knew Craig was just joking around, he felt a flash of anger. He couldn't help retorting, "Well, I helped make our two goals, didn't I? Made you look pretty good, too!"

"Whoa!" said Craig, holding up his hands. "I knew it. There is something eating at you! Don't deny it. Spill it."

"Why?" Mark shot back. "Talking about it won't do any good!"

"Talking about *what*?" Craig pressed.

"About what Vince pulls out there every time we're on the field together!" Mark said finally. "I'm — I'm — I'm just so bugged by that guy! He acts like I'm not even on the team most of the time. But that wouldn't bother me if it weren't for the wisecracks he makes about me. He doesn't — he — he —"

Craig stared at Mark. Then he shook his head and said, "Man, you've got a chip on your shoulder the size of Rhode Island! Did it ever occur to you to confront Vince with this stuff? Just *talk* to the guy, Mark. If you don't let him know where you're coming from, the whole team is going to suffer." He stood up and finished his cup of water. "It's like I tried to tell you before: It's better to talk about it than to keep it all bottled up. I'm gonna get a refill. See you on the bus."

Mark watched him walk away.

Just like that, Mark thought. Just tell someone you have a problem. But what if that someone doesn't hear what you have to say? What then?

For some reason, the image of his parents arguing at the last soccer game flashed through his head.

What then? he thought again.

10

When his grandparents picked him up outside the locker room that night, they had already heard about the game.

"Craig's mother called. She was so excited about him having made a goal," Grandma Conway said. "She said you had a bad fall during the game. Are you okay?"

"It was no big deal," Mark said. He preferred not to remember that that collision with Eddie had mostly been his fault.

"Really? Well, she sounded concerned. In fact, didn't Coach Ryan have you sit out for a while because of the injury?"

Mark squirmed. He wasn't convinced that was why the coach had taken him out of the game. But he didn't want to say as much to his grandparents.

He didn't want to lie, either, though. So he just sat silent for the rest of the ride home and hoped his grandparents would let the matter drop.

They didn't. The minute they walked into the house, Grandpa Conway said, "Young man, you sit down here. Mother, you come sit, too." There was a tone in his voice that told Mark not to argue. He flopped back into his chair and folded his hands.

Grandpa Conway had never acted this way before. There hadn't been one serious talk, the kind his parents used to have with him, since he'd moved back to Knightstown to live with them. Hearing him talk this way reminded Mark that his grandfather was a *father,* too. Mark suddenly wondered what it had been like for his own father growing up here. Somehow, he had a feeling he had been given a much looser rein than his father had had — but that that rein was about to be tightened.

Grandpa Conway cleared his throat. "Now, I'm sure not an expert on what it's like to be a teenager these days," he began, "but I'll bet they're every bit as moody now as they were when your father was growing up. One minute everything's fine; the next it's like the world is about to come crashing down around you. And it's my opinion that most of the time what seems like a mountain to a teenager is really just a molehill."

Grandma Conway nodded. Mark sat silent, not looking at either of them.

Grandpa Conway continued: "However, in your case, I think you're doing just the opposite." Mark's head shot up. His grandfather nodded. "Yes, that's right. Mark, you've got a mountain of turmoil you should be dealing with — but you're trying to pretend it's just a molehill."

"We don't know exactly what happened out on the soccer field today," his grandmother said. "But Mrs. Crandall seemed to think you were about ready to blow your stack at one point. I suppose getting hurt on the field could have been part of the problem. I mean, in the game against the Tigers you fell pretty hard — and neither your grandfather nor I could believe the change that came over you! It was like watching something just boil over."

"But we think something else entirely has been adding fuel to that fire," his grandfather added. "We hoped that you might come to us to talk about it. But you haven't. So now we're going to do what we can to force you to let off some steam."

Mark sat there frozen. He couldn't look at either of his grandparents. His insides were all churned up, and he felt like he was going to break into a million pieces.

He knew his grandparents would wait until he was ready to say something. Finally he decided to tackle the easier problem first.

"I guess I might have been a little angry at some stuff that's been happening on the soccer field," he admitted.

"Is that it?" his grandmother prodded gently.

Mark shrugged.

"What about your mother and father, Mark?" Grandpa Conway said softly. "Doesn't it make you kind of mad that they both keep trying to win you over to their side? Because I don't mind telling you, it makes me mad to watch them do it."

At last Mark looked up. "It does?" he asked.

"You bet it does. I will always love both of them, Mark, but there are times I just want to wring their necks!" Both his grandmother and grandfather smiled ruefully.

"I — I guess it does make me a little angry. I mean," he continued in a louder voice, "I feel like — like — like a soccer ball in the middle of a close game sometimes! Both teams want to get ahold of me, but they have to fight each other to do it! But it's no big deal," he finished, embarrassed by his outburst.

"See, there you go again," said Grandpa Conway. "It *is* a big deal. Your parents are just so busy trying to hurt each other that they don't seem to realize that they're hurting you, too. They should be able to put aside what's bothering them about each other to make things a little nicer, a little easier, for you during this whole thing."

As Mark listened, his eyes filled with tears. They were the first tears he had cried in a long, long time. But it felt good to let it out, he realized. It felt good to be able to talk about all the confusing feelings he'd been trying so hard to ignore for so long.

Grandma Conway got up and came over to him. She crouched down and held him in her arms. "I know," she said, "I know it has to feel real bad. But you can't hold it in or you'll just explode."

"Talk to your mother and father, Mark," said his grandfather. "When you're ready, talk to them and make them listen. Believe me, they've been acting dumb. It's about time they realized it."

Mark gulped. The idea of confronting his parents terrified him, but he knew that his grandparents were right. But still . . .

"Do you really think it'll make a difference? Do you think they'll pay any attention to me if I say something?"

Grandpa Conway looked him square in the eyes. "If you're asking if their feelings for each other will change because of something you say, then no, Mark, I don't think so. But I do know that it'll help you burn up some of that anger you have inside and that it will make them open their eyes a little wider to what they've been doing to you. And that alone will make it worth your while."

With that, he pushed himself up out of his chair and said, "Now, then. Mother, you go put your feet up, and Mark, you get your body into a shower. I'm cooking dinner tonight."

As Mark was toweling off a few minutes later, he realized how right his grandparents were. He did bottle things up too much. Although he was a little embarrassed at having cried in front of them, he knew it had been as cleansing for his emotions as the shower had been for his body. But the situation with his parents was only part of the problem.

Craig hadn't been talking about the same thing as his grandparents, but his message wasn't any different. Some of the anger stored in the depths of Mark's gut had another name on it — and the label read "Vince Loman."

Might as well do a test run there before tackling the big one, Mark thought grimly.

11

Mark had noticed that Vince often rode his bicycle to school. He checked it out on his way into the building the next morning. Sure enough, the bike was in the rack. So, after practice, Mark got cleaned up in record time and waited out near the bike rack for Vince to show up.

It didn't take long. Vince came down the path toting his schoolbooks and gear bag over his shoulder. When he saw Mark near the bike rack, a dark look came over his face, but he didn't say anything.

"I want to talk to you, Vince," said Mark.

"Yeah? Well, I don't have anything to say to you, so just get out of my way."

"Maybe you don't, but I have a lot to say to you." He took hold of the handlebars of Vince's bike. "For one thing, I don't like the way you've been acting toward me."

"Let go of my bike!" Vince snapped. "Or do I have to make you?"

He stood up next to Mark, fists clenched.

Mark took a deep breath but didn't back down.

"Listen," he said. "I'm not leaving until I get some answers out of you. What did I ever do to you? It's like you wish you never laid eyes on me! You treat me like I'm the enemy. I don't care if we never became friends, but I can't pretend that you're not the best soccer player out on that field. I've tried to make things work between us out there, for the sake of the team, but you act like you're playing against me!"

Vince stared at him stonily for what seemed like an hour. Mark was ready to give up, when he finally spoke.

"You say you're playing *with* me," said Vince. "Sounds good, but it isn't like that at all. You're such a good player, you think everyone should do things your way. And you're not quiet about telling them how it should be done, either. You're the new guy on the team, some hotshot from England, so everyone's excited about everything you do. Even the coach, for Pete's sake! You take every chance you can get to show off your skills. From the very first practice, you've been trying to impress everyone. Me? They take *me* for granted. They forget that I'm the one they voted captain last year, that I'm the MVP who led them to an 8-and-3 record!"

Mark stared.

"I don't forget who's captain," he said lamely. "And as for MVP, I just told you I think you're the best player out there."

"Yeah? Well, I'll be surprised if anyone else thinks so. Even when I score a goal, half the time it's because you've set me up. You end up getting as much credit as I do."

"But that's teamwork," Mark protested. "That's what makes for a winning squad. There had to have been someone who set you up all last year, too. What makes what I do out there so different? Don't you know that you and I could be an unstoppable offensive team if we just worked together?"

"And I'm sure you'll be able to outline all kinds of

neat plays for us, thanks to your near-professional experience in England," Vince said nastily.

At that, Mark lost his patience.

"Okay, have it your way! If you're too stupid to see I'm just trying to patch things up between us for the good of the team, then to heck with you! But I can tell you one thing: You have my word on it that I'll be doing my part in each and every play whether it involves you or not. Coach Ryan and the Scorpions deserve that much."

Vince swung a leg over his bike. "You think I don't know that?" Without a backward glance, he pedaled away, leaving Mark standing there.

I hope you do, Mark thought. *But I'm not sure you got what I was talking about.*

He headed over to the bus stop. A few of the guys from the team were already there.

"Hey, Mark, where've you been?" called Charlie Burns. The ruddy-faced Scorpion goalie always had a smile. He was one of the cheeriest guys Mark had ever met.

"Busy signing autographs for the fans?" Mel joked.

"Nah," Craig Crandall joined in. "Mark's been

talking to his talent agent. You know, lining up those TV commercials."

"Oh, right," said Charlie. Then he went on in a deep, husky voice: *"Hi, kids, this is Mark Conway. I always drink three quarts of milk before every game. That's one hundred percent cow juice, and don't get anything else or you'll never be a big star like me."*

Then Mel started in, too. *"If you want to get the kind of job that means you don't have to do any real work, try the Mark Conway home course in soccer and become outstanding in your field."* He stopped and looked at the other boys. "Get it? 'Outstanding in your field?' As in 'Out standing in your field'?"

"Wait a minute, wait a minute!" shouted Craig above the groans. "How about this: *Hi, kiddies, this is Uncle Mark. Have you tried my home workout video? You can have big muscles just like me for only a few dollars a day. Send in for your thirty-day trial right now!"* Craig struck an absurd muscle-man pose.

By now, they were all doubled over with laughter. At first, Mark had still been too steamed to join in the fun. But after a few imitations, even he had to admit his teammates were a bunch of natural comedians. As the bus drove up, he announced good-naturedly, "Okay, you guys, I want to thank you for all your kind endorsements. And I want to tell you about a one-time offer. Play your cards right and you — yes, you — can get to do my math home-work, you — yes, you — can help clean up my room, and you — yes, you — can have my auto-graph for half the going rate!"

"Some deal!"

"A real sport!"

"What a guy!"

The bus took off with a jolt, almost knocking them over like bowling pins. But they were all laughing so hard, no one seemed to notice.

12

Mark arrived at practice the next day with a good feeling. He hoped that some of what he'd said to Vince had sunk in by now. The two of them could lead the team to a league victory if only they could join forces against the opposition.

At first Vince was no different than before. He was icy cold during the warm-up. There was no sign of any change in his attitude. When they were off the field, he ignored Mark completely.

Yet on the field during scrimmage, it was a different story. Plays the coach had outlined weeks before suddenly were working like clockwork. Encouraged, Mark followed his lead as much as possible. Things were far from perfect — but Mark started to think that maybe some of what he had said had hit home for Vince.

That night, the telephone rang just before dinner. Grandma Conway picked it up in the kitchen. A few seconds later, she called out, "Mark, it's for you! Take it on the cordless phone in the living room."

"Okay," he called back. "Oh, hi, Mom. Thanks for getting back to me. I wanted to make sure you're still going to pick me up for this Saturday. . . . You are? Good. . . . No, I'm just looking forward to seeing you, that's all. Oh, and I've got something kind of important to talk to you about. . . . No, I'm not sick or anything. Just don't be late on Saturday, okay? . . . Great. See you then. Bye."

He walked into the kitchen, still holding the phone.

"Did my dad say when he would be back from that business trip?"

"He should be in his office now, I would think," said Grandma Conway.

"Okay if I call him?"

"Go right ahead," she replied. "I'm going to put some potatoes in to bake. Then I'll come work on that puzzle with you."

"Grandma, I haven't done a jigsaw puzzle in weeks!" he said with a smile. "I've been too busy."

107

"Well, then maybe I'll just do one by myself," she said.

"No, I'll help you," Mark said. "I'm not as busy as all that!"

He went back into the living room and dialed his father's office number.

"Dad? It's me, Mark," he said. "Listen, are you still planning to come over here to watch that special on World Cup soccer? . . . You are? Okay, please don't get stuck with something else this time. I really want to watch it with you. And — and there's something else, too. . . . No, I'm fine. I just want to talk to you, okay? . . . Okay, yeah, bye."

He hung up the phone and got out a five-thousand-piece jigsaw puzzle. This ought to take some doing, he thought. He was looking at the puzzle box, but he was thinking about something else entirely.

Saturday morning was unusually warm. But despite the pleasant weather outside, Mark was anything but cheerful. In fact he was a bundle of nerves.

"Now, what are you up to today?" his grandfather asked, picking up the newspaper.

"Uh, well, Dad's coming over to watch that World Cup special later on," said Mark.

Grandma Conway raised an eyebrow. "Isn't your mother coming over this afternoon, too?"

"Uh-huh," said Mark.

"Feel like telling us what's going on?"

Mark shook his head. "But I have a feeling you'll know everything before the afternoon is through."

He left the kitchen without waiting to see their reactions to his announcement.

To kill some time before his parents showed up, Mark decided to clean up his room. He folded all his clothes and shoved the things that went into drawers into drawers. He found hangers and hung up the clothes that were supposed to be hung up.

He cleaned off the top of his chest of drawers and wiped the glass on the pictures of his mother and father that stood on either side of his mirror.

When his parents had first separated, he hadn't wanted to have their pictures out. Looking at them only made him feel bad. But after his talk with his grandparents, he had realized that the pictures weren't what had been causing those hurt feelings.

So he had taken them out again and each night made a point of looking both pictures right in the eyes.

He had just finished relacing his soccer shoes when he heard the doorbell ring.

This is it, he thought, giving the pictures one last glance.

"Mark, your mother is here," Grandma Conway called from below.

"I'll be down in a minute," he called back. Stall, he said to himself. Hang in there. Hope that Grandma Conway will push her into having a cup of tea or something.

He could hear the big old clock in the hallway outside his door ticking away. It sounded like a bomb that was going to explode any minute.

"Mark," his mother's voice rang out. "Are you all right? What's taking so long?"

Before he could come up with an excuse, the telephone rang.

It was picked up in one ring. His grandfather knocked on the door to Mark's bedroom.

"Mark, it's your dad," he said quietly.

He's not coming, flashed through Mark's mind as he took the cordless phone from his grandfather.

"Hello? . . . Hi, Dad," he said, his voice automatically dropping. "What? You're on your car phone? . . . Yes, that's Mom's car. Right, she's here. . . . No, I don't know when she's leaving. That all depends. But what difference does it make? Aren't you coming to be with me?"

There was a long pause while he waited to hear what his father had to say. Finally he breathed a sigh of relief. "Okay, I'll be here."

He left his bedroom and dashed downstairs. Without a word to anyone, he swung open the door and let his father in before the doorbell even rang.

"Come on in, Dad," he said. "Mom, please don't go. I really need to talk to both of you — together."

Grandma and Grandpa Conway quietly retreated into the kitchen and closed the door.

Mark took his father's hand and led him into the living room, where his mother was sitting.

Even with the sun shining through the windows, it felt like the North Pole in there to Mark.

Both of his parents started to speak at the same time.

"Mark, if you're not happy here —"

"Darling, you can come and live with me if you —"

"Stop!" he shouted. "You haven't even listened to me yet. It's not about being here with Grandma and Grandpa Conway. They're terrific, and I love them. They're not the problem."

"Well, then I don't see why we had to be here together to talk about something," said his mother stiffly. "You didn't have to plan this little 'surprise.'"

"Right, if there's something else, you could have let me know about it," said his father.

"Or me," his mother shot back with an angry look at Mr. Conway.

"No, I couldn't!" Mark blurted out. Both his parents turned to stare at him.

"That's just it. Ever since you guys" — Mark's voice broke slightly, but he cleared his throat and continued in a firm voice — "split up, I haven't been able to talk to you about anything. Nothing important, anyway, just about clothes, and school, and how I'm doing on the soccer team. But I've never told either of you my thoughts about what you're doing. About how it makes me feel. I mean, since we're never all together, it always seemed like I'd be talking behind someone's back if I told just one or the other of you. So I just kept it inside. But it's eating me up, so I can't do that anymore," he finished.

His mother spoke first after a long silence. "Darling," she said, "we're not trying to do anything to hurt you. It's just that we can't agree on who you should live with."

"If there was a way to settle the matter without lawyers, we would, Mark," his father added. "But there just isn't."

"So I'm just supposed to pretend it's *okay* that I feel like a soccer ball you two are fighting over?" He could see his angry words were finally sinking in.

"Mark, you never told us you felt like that," his father said, his voice catching.

"Well, now you know. And I know you're doing what's best for you two. But please, stop using me in your game."

He ran out of the room and upstairs to his bedroom.

The house remained quiet for several hours after Mr. and Mrs. Conway left.

Finally, when the sky had begun to darken and the clock's chimes had rung four times, Mark slowly opened his door. He went downstairs into the living room. Grandpa Conway was lighting a fire in the fireplace. Then Grandma Conway came in with a tray of freshly baked lemon squares and a pot of hot chocolate.

"Cocoa?" his grandmother asked, holding up a cup.

Mark took it from her and sat on the arm of her easy chair.

"Thanks, Grandma," he said. She patted his knee and handed him a plate with a lemon square on it.

"You know, I saw in the paper that the Knightstown Cineplex has some good movies," said Grandpa Conway. "There's no school tomorrow, so we could take in one of the early shows. Anyone interested?"

"Fine with me," said Grandma Conway.

They both looked at Mark. He took a long drink of cocoa, bit into a lemon square, and surprised them all, himself included, by saying, "Sure. Why not?"

"Mark," his grandmother admonished without missing a beat, "don't talk with your mouth full."

For some reason, that simple statement made them all laugh.

And for the first time in a long time, Mark didn't feel like he had a heavy weight stuck in his chest. He felt like he could do anything — go to a movie, or play soccer, or even talk with his mouth full — now that he had said what was on his mind.

13

When Mark planted his feet on the soccer field the following week, he felt like a new person. Not all of his problems had gone away — whose ever would? — but he knew he could play now the way he should.

It showed in the very next game the Scorpions played, with the Chelsea Chargers. As usual, the front line started out with Mark, Evan, and Vince. But about ten minutes into the game, Evan got banged up and had to leave. The coach sent in Craig, who had been warming the bench until then.

Craig wasn't a natural forward. He didn't have the speed. So the burden of moving in toward the goal fell pretty much to Mark and Vince.

As soon as the Scorpions had the ball, Vince called for a play they'd practiced all week — except, during practice, Mark had had possession and called the play. Earlier in the season, Mark would have seen this as a ploy by Vince to keep the ball away from him. But now he knew he could count on his teammate to include him. This play depended on each player doing his part in perfect harmony.

"Heads up, Craig!" he shouted as he received the pass from Vince. Vince rushed behind Mark, who turned around and tipped the ball right back to him. Mark then became a blocker as Vince scooted around and headed toward the goal with the ball.

But that wasn't the whole play. Vince had his choice: He could kick for a goal, or pass to either Craig or Mel Duffy. Mark could see that Mel was in the clear. Sure enough, a second later Vince had passed Mel the ball. Mel aimed, swung his leg, and kicked for all he was worth.

The ball sailed into the net for the first goal of the game!

Mark wasn't surprised that Vince didn't come over to slap high fives with him. After all, he thought, I can't expect the guy to change overnight.

The Scorpions took the game against the Chargers, 6–4. Mark and Vince each scored two goals.

Mark knew he and Vince were neck-and-neck for the most goals scored that season. But as far as Mark was concerned, such statistics were unimportant as long as they both did their jobs well.

In the following game, against the Edgewood Eagles, the Scorpions scored five goals before their opponents got on the scoreboard. Final tally: Scorpions 7, Eagles 2. Mark and Vince both sat on the bench, rooting for the substitutes, who played most of the game. But Vince managed to score two more goals to Mark's one nonetheless.

Despite Mark's feelings about in-team competition, he didn't mind the rivalry he and Vince had going. After all, it didn't harm the rest of the squad when their two top scorers were trying to up their records. As long as it didn't spill over to off-field, everything seemed fine.

The Scorpions' record was 8 and 2 when the final game of the season, with the Newtown Panthers, rolled around in mid-November. The Knightstown Scorpions were on top of the league by two games, with the next closest team's record reading 6 and 4.

But Coach Ryan didn't want them to let up just because of that.

"Champions aren't the best only because they've won the most games," he told the Scorpion players just before the game began. "It's because they always play and think like champions. So go out there on the field and show them why Knightstown has earned its spot as number one."

Throughout the season, Coach Ryan had made sure all his players had time on the field. But for this last game, he started with his tried-and-true lineup: Evan, Mark, and Vince on the front line; Jim, Mel, and Johnny at midfield; and Craig, Eddie, Harvey, and Stu in the backfield, with Charlie in the goal.

During the warm-up, Mark glanced at the stands. Sure enough, his grandparents were in their usual place right behind the bench. His parents, however, were nowhere in sight.

Since the day he'd had his say with the two of them in the living room, he was aware of a slight change in the way his parents talked about each other when they were with him. They no longer made angry comments about each other in front of Mark. But Mark knew that sometime soon he was going to become the focus of the divorce again. And what would happen then, he couldn't begin to imagine. Or want to.

For now, he just wanted to concentrate on the game at hand. The Scorpions won the toss. Vince announced that they would start with the ball.

The whistle blew, and the game began. As always, Mark felt a rush of adrenaline as he toed the ball over to Vince, who started to dribble it down along the sideline.

"Come on, you Scorpions!" he shouted, racing to keep pace with Vince. "Let's show 'em how to play this game!"

Within a few moments, it was clear that the Scorpions were the better team. But the Panthers weren't going to simply roll over. They had an impressive record of their own. There was nothing they wanted to do more than end the season by beating the champs.

The Scorpions maintained good ball control and drove in strong to the goal. Passes skittered across the field from Evan to Mark, Mark to Vince, and then back again. But as they approached the goal, the Panthers bared their claws and soon had the ball heading in the opposite direction.

Then Eddie slid beneath a Panther wing and dislodged the ball, booting it out of bounds. The slide scratched him up pretty bad, but he waved away the coach when he asked if he needed to come out. Like everyone else, Eddie was fired up to play the best game he could. Mark knew he wasn't about to let a little scratch send him to the sidelines so soon.

Eddie had his work cut out for him. Mark could see he was having a hard time covering his zone. The Panthers bumped and battered him as he tried to break up their ball control. There was no doubt they were pressing hard to draw "first blood." Twice Eddie got knocked over the sideline as he tried to get a foot around the ball. The third time, though, Mark was right nearby. He bore down on the Panther wing so hard, the surprised player tripped over himself. Eddie ducked in and scooted free with the ball.

His kick downfield was blocked. A Panther interception put the ball back into their control. Then a good block by Harvey Kahn shook the ball loose near Craig. The carrot-topped Scorpion scooped it in, dribbled, then sent it over to Mark.

"Come to Papa!" Mark shouted as he dribbled the ball over the midfield stripe. Looking around, he saw that Vince was up ahead of him, open for a pass. Mark booted it to him. The pass took a wild bounce and rebounded off a Panther's hands. The ref blew his whistle to signal for a direct kick.

Vince was closest and waited for the ref to place the ball. Then he took two large steps and swung his foot hard at the sphere, sending it diagonally across the field. Evan Andrews was already running to get underneath it. With a decisive leap, he headed the ball back toward the center of the field.

Mark wasted no time. He rushed forward, caught the spinning ball against his chest, and let it drop to the ground. Out of the corner of his eye, he saw Vince streaking down the sideline. Mark knew Vince's next move was going to be to cut across the field. He'd be looking for a clean pass.

Now was the Scorpions' chance. It was up to Mark to make it work.

He did. A swift movement sent the ball rocketing to Vince. Vince controlled the ball, turned, and threaded the needle by hooking a kick just beyond the outstretched arms of the Panther goalie.

Score! Scorpions 1, Panthers 0.

Mark could see Coach Ryan smiling as he pounded his right fist into his left palm. He knew the coach loved to see a goal result from teamwork, not just from a fluke.

The next time the Scorpions had possession of the ball, Mark hoped he'd get a shot at scoring. He could tell his teammates were looking to set him up.

He didn't disappoint them. He trapped the ball, dribbled, passed, and positioned himself exactly the way they had practiced all week. So he was in just the right spot to go for it when his moment came.

He didn't have to wait long. A pass from Mel a few feet from the corner of the penalty area was all it took. The Panther goalie never had a chance.

Goal!

Less than halfway through the first half, and already the Scorpions had a solid lead.

The sweet thought of a shutout drifted through Mark's mind, but he quickly blocked it out. That was dangerous, he knew. The idea was to win the game, not to think about a particular score.

Unfortunately the rest of the team didn't see it that way. The lead went to their heads, and play got sloppy. A lot of kicking, tripping, and pushing fouls led to one penalty after another. The Panthers didn't hesitate to use these lucky breaks. When the whistle blew to end the first half, the score was tied: Scorpions 2, Panthers 2.

Coach Ryan had a good long talk with his team during the break.

"What is going on out there?" he asked incredulously. "You'd think it was the first game of the season instead of the last! You have one final chance to show why you're the champs. Now, go out there and show those guys who's boss! Let's see some clean, smart, heads-up ball!"

With a roar, the Scorpions took to the field. But Mark sensed that the Panthers could smell an upset.

Well, they're going to have to earn it. We're not about to give it to them on a silver platter, he thought with determination.

The second half of the game turned into a defensive duel. Back and forth, up and down the field, the ball traveled as the referee's time clock ground away the remaining minutes left to play.

Neither team managed to put the ball into the net for a score. Each of them came close, but their defense came through every time.

Any rivalry that had existed between Mark and Vince vanished as they tried to make one play after another work. But to no avail. The Panthers just seemed to be everywhere, blocking every kick, intercepting every pass.

Then, after a long siege defending the Scorpion goal, Charlie Burns managed to clear the ball out to Vince. Vince broke loose from the Panther defending him and dribbled the ball across the midfield line. When he started to get into trouble, he booted the ball to Jim, who sent it immediately over to Mark.

Mark knew the game was going to end at any moment. He had only one chance to break the tie. But his line to the goal was blocked by a jungle of Panthers.

Suddenly he remembered a play that the team hadn't used in weeks. It was a simple enough play, involving only two players. But those two players had to be able to read each other's minds in order to make it work. One misstep, and that would be that.

Still, Mark figured it was their best shot against this difficult defense.

"Scorpion Red!" he called out. He prayed Vince had heard him. And would do what he had to do without a second thought.

He had. He did. When Mark passed him the ball, Vince trapped it, then kicked it high over the Panthers' heads in a graceful arc. While the Panthers were watching it, Mark darted in between them. He didn't need to keep an eye on it to know where it was going to fall. He just had to be there when it did.

The Panthers' goalie stepped out of the goal, readying himself to catch the ball. And that's when Mark the Scorpion struck.

He gave a mighty sideways leap and headed the ball right over the goalie's outstretched arms. Unable to stop himself from falling, he struck the ground hard and felt the breath knocked right out of him.

But the cheers from the stands made him forget his pain. He didn't even need to look at the score-board to know that the play had succeeded.

Within seconds of the ref blowing the whistle that ended the game, a sea of fans poured onto the field and completely surrounded the Scorpions. Mark looked up from where he lay to see Vince holding out a hand to help him up.

Just then, Grandma and Grandpa Conway gingerly made their way over to him.

"That was the most exciting play I've ever seen!" said Grandma Conway, rubbing her mittened hand behind his neck as she drew him close. Grandpa Conway clapped him on the back and kept repeating, "Wonderful! Wonderful!"

Mark tried to free himself to find Vince in the crowd to offer his congratulations and thanks. But the right wing was nowhere in sight.

The following Monday, Coach Ryan held a meeting of the Scorpions during their regular practice time.

"All right, guys, settle down," he said. "We have a few things to do to wind up the season. First, it's the tradition here at Knightstown Middle School to elect next year's captain at the close of the previous season. This should be someone who is willing to take on the job and has shown leadership abilities out on the field. Okay, the floor is open for nominations."

Charlie Burns's hand shot up. "I nominate Vince Loman."

"Does anyone second the nomination?"

Stu Watts seconded.

"Any other nominations?"

Craig spoke up: "I nominate Mark Conway."

"I second Mark," Mel added.

Mark was pleased to be nominated, but he was a little concerned, too. He'd taken it for granted that Vince would get the job again. If Mark was elected, would that put an end to their truce?

"Well, since there don't appear to be any other nominations, let's vote. Unless the nominees would like to say a few words first?"

Vince shook his head.

"Mark?" asked the coach.

Mark was about to shake his head, too. But something got into him and he changed his mind.

"I'm happy just to be a member of the team," he said. "But if I can help out by being the captain, I'd be proud to do it."

"All right, then," said the coach. He handed out little slips of paper to each player.

For a moment, everyone was busy writing down a name. Then the coach collected them in his cap.

Mark looked up, expected the coach to figure out the tally right then and there. But he didn't.

"It's also a tradition here to announce the captain at the awards banquet being held this Saturday night. So Vince, Mark, you'll just have to sit tight until then!"

The boys all laughed at Mark's surprised look. Mark wondered if Vince was as uncomfortable about hearing the winner in such a public way as he was. But traditions were traditions, after all.

14

Craig and Mark were seated in the backseat of the Crandalls' station wagon. Mr. and Mrs. Crandall were driving them to the Scorpions' awards banquet. Both boys were dressed up in their best clothes.

"Stop messing around with those neckties," Mrs. Crandall said over her shoulder. "You both look very nice, so just leave things that way."

"How are your grandparents getting to the banquet?" asked Craig.

"My dad's picking them up," said Mark. After a moment, he added, "My mom's going to be there, too. She's sitting with Evan's parents."

"Cool," said Craig. And that was that. No probing questions about the situation. Craig just accepted it for what it was.

Which is what I'm slowly learning to do, Mark thought.

Craig elbowed him. "Got your acceptance speech all written?" he asked with a grin.

"Cut it out," Mark said, blushing.

"Why? You're the best person on the team to be captain, and everyone knows it. Announcing it at the banquet is just a formality."

Mark wasn't so sure. "I don't know. Vince is a terrific player. And besides, he's grown up with you guys. I hear that he was always the leader, even in kindergarten."

But Craig just said, "We'll see," and left it at that.

When the car stopped, the boys hopped out and ran off to join their pals.

The Knightstown Middle School gymnasium was all decked out with scarlet and gray streamers. Hanging from the ceiling was a big banner that spelled out, KNIGHTSTOWN SCORPIONS — CHAMPIONSHIP TEAM.

A few tables near the stage had signs on them that read, RESERVED FOR TEAM. Mark and Craig scrambled to get good seats so that they could watch the presentations after dinner. They were joined by Stu, Eddie, Mel, Willie, and Charlie. The rest of the tables filled just as quickly.

"Yuck, I hate those squishy grapes they put in these things," said Craig, pointing to the fruit cup in front of him.

"Give it to Charlie," advised Mel. "He'll swallow anything that doesn't move."

The guys all laughed and began to eat their dinners. After they had finished off three baskets of rolls, their chicken, mashed potatoes, peas, and the apple pie with vanilla ice cream, they were ready for the awards.

The coach got up on stage and stood in front of the microphone.

"I want to thank everyone for coming here tonight to honor a great bunch of athletes. Every one of them deserves an award for just getting out there and doing his best. I'm proud of them and hope you will all join me in a round of applause for the Knightstown Middle School Scorpions."

Everyone in the gym applauded, long and loud. The members of the team tried not to look dumb, but they couldn't help smiling at one another.

Then the coach called them up on stage, one by one, to receive their team letters. They were big scarlet-and-gray *K*'s. Printed over each one was a cartoon scorpion on top of a black-and-white soccer ball.

"Next," Coach Ryan said, "I'd like to present the award for Most Improved Performance. This award goes to a returning player who has shown the most improvement from the previous year. And this year, the award goes to . . . Charlie Burns!"

Charlie climbed the stairs to the stage and took a package from the coach. He stepped to the microphone and mumbled, "Uh, thanks. I — I — I'll keep trying."

When he got back to the table, the guys made him open the package. Inside was a video of that year's World Cup finals.

"Wow! It sure pays to get better!" exclaimed Craig.

"Something to go for next year," agreed Mark.

On stage, the coach held up a silver trophy cup. "This award," he said, "belongs to the team's Most Valuable Player. That player's name will be added to the others inscribed on the trophy's base. Then the trophy will be placed back in the case at the entrance of the school, where all can see it. This year, the award goes to . . ."

He paused and looked down at the tables filled with members of the team. Craig nudged Mark's knee and gave his pal a knowing look. But Mark just shook his head.

"Vince Loman!"

The gymnasium exploded in applause. Everyone got up to cheer as Vince accepted his award. Finally the coach asked people to please sit down. Then he pointed at the microphone and nodded to Vince.

Mark expected Vince to be as brief as Charlie. But instead, Vince took a piece of paper from his shirt pocket and stared at it a moment. Then he started to speak.

"I want to thank Coach Ryan and all the Scorpions. Without all of you, I wouldn't have been such a good player this year. It was an honor to be your captain and to be chosen as MVP."

There, that was a nice speech, Mark thought. Whoever would have figured that Vince could speak like that?

But Vince hadn't finished.

"As many of you probably know, I won this award last year, too. But I have to tell you, it wasn't so tough then. This time, I worked much harder than I ever did before out there on the field. This time, I really feel like I earned the award. You see, someone at dinner here tonight — someone on the team, that is — pushed me to be the best player I could be. I'm not even sure he knows it, but it made a real difference. In fact," Vince continued, glancing briefly at Coach Ryan, "it seems that player made a real impression on most all of us. Because he's the one we elected to be our captain next year. Heck, I even voted for him myself — and I was one of the nominees! Mark Conway, congratulations!"

This time, the applause was deafening. Mark just sat there, stunned as much by what Vince had said as he was by the way his election had been announced. Then he broke into a large grin.

When the noise died down, Coach Ryan said, "I want to thank everyone for coming here tonight and for your support all season. Now, drive carefully and we'll see you all next year!"

As the banquet broke up, people came by to congratulate Mark, Vince, and Charlie. Mark spied his grandparents and parents standing by the doorway. But before he slipped away to join them, he turned to Vince.

"Congratulations, Mr. MVP!" he said, stretching out his hand.

Vince took it immediately and shook it. "And to you, too, Captain," he said with a smile.

"That was really nice, what you said up there," Mark said.

"I meant it," Vince replied. "You really did push me, and it was good for me. And you are the best man for the captain's job because you're always thinking about the good of the team. I — I think I lost sight of that for a while."

Mark didn't say anything. But he knew that he was already looking forward to the next season, when he and Vince would *really* be playing on the same team.

He caught up to his family a moment later. They all congratulated him warmly. Then his mother turned to his father and said, "So next Tuesday, then?"

His father nodded curtly. His mother bent down,

gave Mark a quick kiss and a hug, then said she had to be on her way.

Mr. Conway left to find the car to take Grandma, Grandpa, and Mark back home.

"What's next Tuesday?" Mark asked while he was gone.

His grandparents exchanged glances. Grandma Conway sighed and said, "Next Tuesday is the day you have to meet with the judge. She wants to talk with you about your parents' divorce."

15

Your father wanted to pick you up," Mark's grandfather said Tuesday morning. "But your grandmother and I are going to the courthouse anyway, so you might as well ride there with us."

Mark didn't say anything. In fact, ever since the ride home from the banquet, he hadn't felt much like talking.

In the car, he sat up front with his grandfather. Once again, he was dressed in his best clothes.

Mark had never been inside the Knightstown courthouse before. It was a really old building. If it weren't for his parents fighting over who he was to live with and for how long, he might have found it interesting, he supposed. It had marble floors and shiny oak walls. The whole place smelled as though it had just been polished.

138

But all he wanted was to get things over with so he could get out of there.

His mother and father each gave him a hug and a kiss when he saw them. Then they went off and talked with their lawyers in separate parts of the courthouse. He sat with his grandparents on a hard bench. And waited.

Finally someone dressed like a policeman came and told them that Judge Wilkerson was ready. They followed him into the judge's chambers.

When he came in with his grandparents, Judge Wilkerson smiled at him and asked him to sit down on a couch next to her. His parents were already sitting in big chairs facing the couch. His grandparents remained standing.

"There, now," said the judge. "I think we can start. Will everybody but Mark and Mr. and Mrs. Conway please leave? I'll let you know when we're ready for you to come back. Please wait outside in case there's anything I need to ask you."

The lawyers and Mark's grandparents left the room.

Judge Wilkerson spoke directly to Mark.

"First, let's go over why we're here," she said.

Then she went on to explain that Mark's parents had decided to get a divorce because they had personal problems they couldn't solve. She pointed out again and again that these problems had nothing to do with their feelings for Mark. Did he understand?

Mark nodded slowly.

"Fine," said the judge. "Then what we need to figure out is what's best for you."

Mark nodded again, then cleared his throat. "Excuse me," he said. "But if you don't mind, may I speak?"

"By all means," said the judge. "It's important to hear what you have to say about this."

"I know that you want to decide which of my parents get to have me," Mark said to the judge. "And I want them to know that I love them both very much. But for a long time, I've felt like the rope in a tug-of-war." He paused and looked at his parents. "Mom, you yourself told me your company might be moving soon and that you hoped you would still be part of their team if they did. And Dad, your company is always transferring you all over the place — even across the Atlantic Ocean!

"The moving around didn't bother me so much

a few years ago. But now I have a real home. I go to the Middle School, and I have lots of friends. I'm on the soccer team, and I just got elected captain. I like it here. And I like living with my grandparents."

The judge looked a little surprised. "You do?" she asked.

"Yes," Mark answered. "They're old, but they really make an effort. They went to almost all my games. They know my friends' names. And they talk to me about what's happening to me in school and everything." He smiled briefly. "They talk to me like parents sometimes, too. They're the ones who made me realize that ignoring my feelings wasn't doing me any good."

The judge smiled with him.

"I love my mom and dad," Mark continued. "But I'm tired of moving, and I'm tired of making new friends. Mom and Dad, you both lived in Knightstown before, so you know it's a good place for me to grow up, right?"

His parents both nodded. His mother opened her mouth to speak, but Mark stopped her.

"If nobody minds too much, I have to be honest.

And if Grandma and Grandpa wouldn't mind, I'd like to leave things just as they are."

When he was through, he couldn't look up at his folks. He stared down at the carpet as the judge spoke to him.

"Mark, would you mind leaving me alone with your parents for a few minutes?" she said.

Without a word, Mark stood up and left the room.

When he got outside, Grandma and Grandpa Conway went to him and took him by the hand. They didn't say anything. The three of them just sat back on the same bench as before.

It seemed like hours went by before the judge herself appeared and called them back into her chambers.

Mr. and Mrs. Conway were now seated together side by side on the couch. Mrs. Conway's eyes were red and puffy, and Mark's father kept wiping his nose with his handerchief.

The judge turned to Grandma and Grandpa Conway.

"Are you willing to let Mark stay with you a little longer?" she asked.

His grandparents looked astonished. But they

didn't hesitate in answering. "We would like nothing more," Grandma Conway said. Grandpa Conway nodded his agreement.

"All right, then," said the judge. "I'm going to postpone my decision for a period of no more than a year. During that time, Mark will remain living with his grandparents. Mr. and Mrs. Conway, your lawyers will contact you in the near future to arrange another meeting to discuss this subject. In the meantime, I suggest you both try to settle your work lives in such a way that, should the court decide in your favor, you will be able to provide a stable, loving home for Mark."

And that was that.

"You really don't have to leave?" Craig asked for the third time that afternoon.

Mark laughed and kicked the soccer ball through a pile of leaves to him. "For the last time, you're not getting rid of me that easily!"

"Okay, guys, enough chitchat! Let's get that ball moving!" came a voice from behind them.

Mark whirled around in time to see Vince stealing the ball right out from under Craig's nose.

"Drat!" said Craig. "I'm never going to earn that Most Improved Player award next year!"

The three boys collapsed into laughter. Then, with the crisp November air filling their lungs, they headed out onto the playground field to take advantage of the last lingering rays of afternoon sun.

Matt Christopher®

Sports Bio Bookshelf

Muhammad Ali	Randy Johnson
Lance Armstrong	Michael Jordan
Kobe Bryant	Peyton and Eli Manning
Jennifer Capriati	Yao Ming
Dale Earnhardt Sr.	Shaquille O'Neal
Jeff Gordon	Albert Pujols
Ken Griffey Jr.	Jackie Robinson
Mia Hamm	Alex Rodriguez
Tony Hawk	Babe Ruth
Ichiro	Curt Schilling
LeBron James	Sammy Sosa
Derek Jeter	Tiger Woods

THE #1 SPORTS SERIES FOR KIDS

MATT CHRISTOPHER ®

Read them all!

- Baseball Flyhawk
- Baseball Turnaround
- The Basket Counts
- Body Check
- Catch That Pass!
- Catcher with a Glass Arm
- Catching Waves
- Center Court Sting
- Centerfield Ballhawk
- Challenge at Second Base
- The Comeback Challenge
- Comeback of the Home Run Kid
- Cool as Ice
- The Diamond Champs
- Dirt Bike Racer
- Dirt Bike Runaway

- Dive Right In
- Double Play at Short
- Face-Off
- Fairway Phenom
- Football Double Threat
- Football Fugitive
- Football Nightmare
- The Fox Steals Home
- Goalkeeper in Charge
- The Great Quarterback Switch
- Halfback Attack*
- The Hockey Machine
- Hot Shot
- Ice Magic
- Johnny Long Legs
- Karate Kick

*Previously published as Crackerjack Halfback

The Kid Who Only Hit Homers

Lacrosse Face-Off

Lacrosse Firestorm

Line Drive to Short**

Long-Arm Quarterback

Long Shot for Paul

Look Who's Playing First Base

Miracle at the Plate

Mountain Bike Mania

Nothin' But Net

Penalty Shot

Power Pitcher***

The Reluctant Pitcher

Return of the Home Run Kid

Run for It

Shoot for the Hoop

Shortstop from Tokyo

Skateboard Renegade

Skateboard Tough

Slam Dunk

Snowboard Champ

Snowboard Maverick

Snowboard Showdown

Soccer Duel

Soccer Halfback

Soccer Hero

Soccer Scoop

Stealing Home

The Submarine Pitch

The Team That Couldn't Lose

Tennis Ace

Tight End

Top Wing

Touchdown for Tommy

Tough to Tackle

Wingman on Ice

The Year Mom Won the Pennant

All available in paperback from Little, Brown and Company
**Previously published as Pressure Play
***Previously published as Baseball Pals